'Look,' he said, 'there's the blue sea in front of you, land there in the distance. The sun is shining, you can smell the sea air, feel the wind on your skin. Why do you want to live in London, Abbey?'

'Mostly because that's where my work is. And it's a great city. Haven't you ever lived in a city?'

'Once or twice, but I've always been glad to move on. I'll be pleased when I move on from here—there'll be something new over the horizon.'

Abbey didn't want to hear this. If he moved on from Dunlort, would he move on from her? Then she remembered. She had determined for a while to live for the day.

Gill Sanderson aka Roger Sanderson, started writing as a husband-and-wife team. At first Gill created the storyline, characters and background, asking Roger to help with the actual writing. But her job became more and more time-consuming and he took over all of the work. He loves it! Roger has written many Medical Romance™ books for Harlequin Mills & Boon®. Ideas come from three of his children—Helen is a midwife, Adam a health visitor, Mark a consultant oncologist. Weekdays are for work; weekends find Roger walking in the Lake District or Wales.

Recent titles by the same author:

TELL ME
YOU LOVE ME

BY
GILL SANDERSON

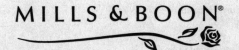

MILLS & BOON®

To Pat T., most helpful of librarians

First published in Great Britain 2006
Harlequin Mills & Boon Limited,
Eton House, 18-24 Paradise Road, Richmond, Surrey TW9 1SR

© Gill Sanderson 2006

ISBN 0 263 84711 X

Set in Times Roman 10½ on 13¼ pt.
03-0206-46823

Printed and bound in Spain
by Litografia Rosés, S.A., Barcelona

CHAPTER ONE

SOMEONE was invading her space!

So far it had all been marvellous. Her old free-diving skills hadn't deserted her and the water was just the right temperature. Out of sheer exhilaration she had turned a couple of back flips. She had glided through a forest of waving seaweed, the fronds brushing her body. An easy thrust to the surface, lungful of air and down again.

This time she was relaxed, not moving, arms floating by her sides, about twenty feet from the surface. For a few seconds it was pleasant just to hang there in a world with no gravity. She was supported, gently rocked, by the sea. Then behind her she felt the unmistakable eddy that suggested that another diver was close by. But she wanted this lonely cove to herself!

Before she could turn to see who was approaching her, an arm was passed around her chest, crushing her breasts, grasping her under her armpit. She was pulled back against someone's chest, felt the powerful thrust of legs beating against hers, his spare arm pulling down at the water. Someone was dragging her to the surface! And she wasn't ready to go.

Well, if he was taking her to the surface, without asking her permission, he could do all the work himself. She wasn't going to kick to help him. She could have felt angry. But like all divers she had learned to control her feelings, to make no sudden movements or decisions, to keep calm. It was the only way to survive underwater.

She was certain that it was a man. A woman would have at least swum round to the front to establish eye contact. And the power of the kicks suggested that it was a man.

With a splash they broke the surface. Whoever it was now supported her with just one arm, and reached for her mask. Well, it was time to assert herself a little.

Of course, she had guessed what he had been doing. He must have thought she had passed out underwater, had decided to drag her to the surface. Well, that had been good of him. But he should have checked with her first.

She started to kick now, a slow lazy stroke that, with the added area of her fins, was more than enough to keep her head above water. She raised her arm and made the universal diver's signal that she was OK—her thumb and forefinger forming a circle.

The arm disappeared from her back. And she was facing her would-be rescuer.

It *was* a man. As she looked at him he pushed his hair out of his eyes, shook his head so that droplets of water scattered about them. It was difficult to decide what a man looked like when he was wet. He was a little older than her—perhaps in his early thirties. His skin was tanned, his eyes were the darkest blue she had ever seen. And his voice shook with controlled anger.

'Don't you know that it's not safe to dive on your own? You could have been killed.' His voice was harsh.

Abbey would take lessons on diving safety from no one. She suspected she was just as expert as this man.

She snapped, 'First, I was free-diving, I didn't have an air cylinder on my back. Second, I've ten years' experience of this, I know what's safe and what isn't. Third, I checked with the locals, they assured me that this cove was safe.'

'You were down far too long!'

'I know how long I can stay under. I've practised, I'm trained. And I didn't hyperventilate.'

Too many people who were new to diving thought that before swimming underwater they should breathe in and out deeply, try to draw oxygen into the bloodstream. But hyperventilation was dangerous. It could cause people to lose consciousness without realising it.

The man still wasn't convinced she was safe. 'And when I came in after you, you were just hanging there. You looked unconscious.'

Well, yes, she had to admit that could be true. 'Sometimes I like to relax just for a few seconds let the water do what it wants with me. Don't you do that?'

'No. A man should never forget that he does not belong under water.'

'Neither should a woman,' said Abbey sharply.

Only now did she notice that the man wasn't dressed for diving—or swimming. She could see the neck of a white polo shirt, and when she ducked her mask under-water she saw that he was wearing dark jeans. His feet were bare. 'You thought I was in trouble and you just dived in after me,' she said. 'You did pretty well to pull me up from that depth, without fins.'

'I train a lot.'

'Well, I might have needed you, so thanks for the thought. I'm sorry your clothes are wet.'

'They'll dry,' he said laconically. 'Are you going to carry on diving alone?'

She would have liked to, for a few minutes more. But it seemed rather ill-mannered after this man had possi-bly ruined his clothes for her. 'I guess I've had enough,' she said. 'Back to shore?'

He rolled over, set off for the pebbly beach at a speed that Abbey found surprising. She was an experienced swimmer herself, she had the great advantage of fins on her feet, but she couldn't keep up with him. He had said—mockingly of course—that he trained. He'd been telling the truth.

She reached the shore just after him, stood knee-deep in the waves to pull off her fins. Then she took off her mask and went to speak to her would-be rescuer.

As she walked up the beach she saw him cross his arms and pull his wet shirt over his head. He twisted the shirt to wring the surplus water out, and Abbey blinked as she saw the ripple of muscles across his chest, shoul-ders and arms. She was a doctor, she had seen the bod-ies of many fit men. But this one was the perfect male animal.

She looked more closely. The large, dark blue eyes gave just a touch of softness to his face. Otherwise the high cheekbones, craggy brow and now thin mouth made him seem more menacing than ever.

'Dr Abbey Fraser?'

Abbey stared at him. 'Yes. How did you know my name?'

'I came here to find you.'

Abbey looked around the lonely cove, and couldn't help feeling a thrill of apprehension.

Not three hours ago she had turned off the main road to Aberdeen and had headed for the sea, for the little Scots port of Dunlort. She had parked on the top of the hill looking down on the port, stepped out of the car and for the first time had smelt the sea air. It had been good.

She had felt hot and sticky. It had been a long drive from London but now it all seemed worthwhile. She needed to be out of the City, away from the hospital, free from the noise and the smell and the pressure. She needed a new life, and perhaps this would be the start.

For the past eighteen months she had worked full time in A and E at the hospital and had also managed to look after her father, watching his slow but inevitable decline. She had been happy to give up any thought of a social life. But now he was dead and although she had wept bitterly Abbey had to admit that his death had been a blessing.

And two years ago her husband had died. But... Abbey shrugged. That had been another story.

Now was to be a new start. She needed a life.

She looked at the port below her. There was the harbour and moored to two buoys was a converted trawler—Abbey guessed it was the *Hilda Esme*. It looked serviceable, seaworthy. That ship was going to be her workplace and often her home for the next six or eight weeks.

It was two days before she was expected to report for duty. She had booked into a hotel and would spend a while looking around the area, perhaps do some walking. Already she felt that this place would be like balm to her soul.

Abbey slid back into her car, drove down to Dunlort to start her new life.

Her hotel room was comfortable. She put out her photographs, of her father and her brother and two nieces. Her brother's family lived in Florida, but they were a close family and were in constant contact. She connected her laptop, no e-mails since her early leaving this morning. Then she looked out of the window at the gorgeous blue sea, decided that she just had to have a swim.

'Walk about a mile south along the beach,' the hotel proprietor told her. 'There's a rocky cove there that's beautiful for diving. If you see a lobster, bring it back.'

'And it's quite safe?'

'Yes, it's safe. I used to be a fisherman, I know all the waters round here. But you have been diving before?' He was obviously concerned

'I'm trained. And I'm going to be the doctor for the divers on the *Hilda Esme*,' Abbey said.

The hotel proprietor nodded. 'That sounds good enough for me.'

She packed her fins and mask, the rest of her kit, even her dry suit. She was there to work but there might be a chance to get below, to have a real dive. Who could tell? She was starting a new life.

But apparently she was starting her new life by having an argument with an angry and menacing man.

'How do you know my name?'

He seemed to be aware of her apprehension. He smiled, and suddenly he wasn't menacing. The smile altered him completely. It made her feel that he was her friend and she wanted to be his friend. He spread his damp shirt on a rock so it could dry, and that simple task made him even less frightening.

'Don McBeth, the man at the hotel who told you about this place, gave me your name. He thought perhaps I might want to talk to you. And I did. I do.'

'You want to talk to me?'

He moved towards her, offered her his hand. 'We're going to work together. You're Dr Abbey Fraser, the doctor who will be looking after the divers on the *Hilda Esme*. I'm John Cameron. I'm dive master on the ship.'

That was unexpected. Still, she took his hand. 'Good to meet you, John.'

His grip on her hand was firm but not painful. She had met too many men who tried to assert their masculinity by squeezing her fingers. This man didn't need to.

'I'm sorry if I was a bit ill-mannered earlier,' he said, 'and it must have been a shock for you, being grabbed from behind and dragged up to the surface. But I'm a dive master and I tend to get a bit paranoid about safety.'

'It's a good fault,' she said.

Then it struck her that she was having an amiable conversation with a half-naked man, and that she was clad only in a bathing suit. True, they were on a beach but... She walked to where her clothes were piled on a rock, took the towel and threw it to him. 'You can dry your hair if you want,' she said.

He shrugged, tossed the towel back. 'I'll drip dry,' he said. 'Besides, the sun is warm. But you get dressed and then we can walk back to town together.'

There was a convenient rock for her to change behind, so she wriggled out of her costume, back into shorts and shirt. She'd have a shower as soon as she got back to the hotel. But for now she did what she could with her short hair, even thought of putting on a dab of lipstick. Perhaps not. She stuffed her wet things into the bag she had brought.

She came from behind her rock. John had his back to her and was sitting on another rock, looking out to sea. For a quick moment she admired the powerful latissimus dorsi muscles of his back, curving down to a trim waist. She looked at his profile. He was staring at a ship far out to sea, a half-smiling expression on his face that she recognised but couldn't quite place. Then she reminded herself that she was to be this man's doctor. She went and sat beside him—but not too close.

'Have you worked on the *Hilda Esme* long?' she asked.

'No. I've been working for the firm for just a week. An agency got me the job.'

'And you're a professional dive master?'

He shrugged again. 'Diver, dive master. Wherever there's work, I'll go there. In fact, at times, as well as the diving, I'll be working directly for you. I trained as a navy paramedic, I'm supposed to give you a hand if you need it.'

'You're not working for me, you're working with me. And I've worked with navy-trained paramedics before, their training is brilliant.' She thought for a minute and then said, 'At the interview for this job I was told that there was a hyperbaric chamber on board and that there was a technician who could maintain it. Don't tell me that's you as well?'

He laughed. 'That's me. Jack of all trades. I also maintain the compressor that fills the air tanks.'

It was pleasant to sit there in the sun, she thought, having a leisurely professional conversation. There was none of the frantic hurry of her old job, the sense that if things weren't done at once, they'd never be done. And she sensed she was going to like working with John.

'I hope you're not going to give me any grief about this not being a woman's job,' she said.

'No. If you can do it, then I'm happy with a woman doctor. What's more—and I don't think there will be— if there's any trouble from the men, I'll sort it.'

She smiled. 'No, John. I'll sort it. If I can't cope, I'll leave.'

'I suspect that you'll cope. They're not a bad bunch

of lads.' He hesitated. 'May I ask…how come you became a divers' doctor?'

'I was—I am—an amateur diver. I was a doctor, and I became accredited to specialise in diving medicine.'

She thought for a moment, decided to tell him. 'They don't really need a doctor for this job, a trained paramedic such as yourself would do just as well. I could earn twice as much working in A and E. But I needed a change. And it's only for a few weeks.'

'I like short jobs,' he said. Then he looked down at her hands and frowned. 'Is your finger itching? You've not been bitten or anything? A jellyfish?'

She looked down and frowned herself. It had been an unconscious action and she was annoyed.

'It's my ring finger,' she said. 'Until a month ago I wore a wedding ring.'

'You were married? Now divorced? Don't tell me if you don't want to, I don't want to pry.'

She hesitated, and then said, 'I was married but my husband is dead. It was some time ago, and the marriage was pretty rocky anyway. I'm not grieving or anything. I don't want to think about the past. I'm living for now.'

'Sounds reasonable. Why did you keep your ring on for so long?'

'My father was ill, I spent all my spare time looking after him. I worked in a hospital and wearing a wedding ring meant I wasn't plagued by men wanting a date.'

'And your father is OK now?'

'He died a few weeks ago. Just. I miss him no end,

but I've got to start my new life.' It took an effort to tell him this. Her father's death still affected her.

John nodded. 'I'm sorry for your loss,' he said. 'But I think you've got the right idea. Start a new life, don't live in the past. The future will sort itself out.'

He stood, stretched, and once again Abbey had to look away from the play of muscles across his chest. It was…disturbing.

He said, 'Been good to talk to you, Abbey, but I've got work to do. All the equipment on the ship has been serviced, but I need to know it's been done properly so I've been working my way through it all, checking that everything is up to standard.'

Abbey nodded. She had met this kind of obsession before among divers. Kit was constantly examined and re-examined. That's the way they ensured they stayed alive.

'I think I'll stay here in the sun and read for a while,' she said. 'I'm not due to start officially for a couple of days but I'll phone the captain and let him know I'm here. I'm glad we've met, John, and I'm looking forward to working with you.' She grinned. 'And I promise not to go back in the water when you've gone.'

'Good. You should always have a buddy when you dive.'

He crammed his feet into a pair of old espadrilles, slung the damp shirt over his shoulders. He looked a little nervous.

'I usually have a drink last thing at night,' he said. 'There's a bar on the harbour, called the Lost Ship, that's where the divers meet. I thought I'd have to keep an eye on them, make sure no one overdid things, but they're pretty good.'

'Last thing you want is a diver with a hangover,' Abbey said.

'Don't tell me. Anyway, would you like to come and have a drink and meet the lads? Or could I come up to your hotel and we could have a drink in the bar there? We're going to have to work together so perhaps it's a good idea for us to get to know each other.' He added, 'If you want a drink, that is. You might be tired.'

She liked the way he had given her an excuse if she wanted one, a reason for not having a drink. It showed sensitivity. And she was tired but… 'Get to know each other?' she asked with a smile. 'You mean as colleagues rather than as man and woman?'

'It could be both—or either,' he said.

It would be more sensible to wait a day or two before having a drink with this man. She hardly knew him, they would have to work together and… But she was starting a new life.

'See you at the bar of my hotel,' she said. 'Just for the last hour.'

'I'll look forward to that.' And he was gone. She watched him walk along the beach until he was out of sight.

Hmm, she thought. My new life seems to be starting quickly.

She had brought a book with her as she had intended to sit in the sun and read for a couple of hours—she had even brought her suncream. But she couldn't settle.

Eventually she slung her bag over her shoulder and looked around. There was an overgrown path running from her little cove to the top of the cliffs. She'd go up there and explore.

There was an even more overgrown path along the top of the cliffs. She followed it, happy for a while just to walk and to wonder at the scenery. She had her digital camera with her and took photographs of the cliffs, the birds, the sea. Later that day she'd download them onto her laptop, and then send copies to her family in Florida.

After fifteen minutes or so she turned a corner and there was the perfect picture. A ruined castle on a headland, surrounded on three sides by sea and accessible only by a dubious-looking bridge. It was so romantic, so beautiful. Abbey unslung her bag, groped for her camera—and kicked the bag over the edge of the path.

Dismayed, she watched it tumble downwards a few feet, bounce over a ledge and disappear out of sight in a thicket of gorse. That would teach her to go wild over a ruined castle!

Perhaps all was not lost. The cliff here wasn't sheer, it was steep but covered with scrub. If she was careful she ought to be able to scramble down and retrieve her bag. She certainly wasn't going to abandon it. Thrusting her camera into the pocket of her shorts, she stepped off the path.

She discovered that there once might have been a bit of a path downwards. There were a couple of helpful stones to balance on, a step cut into the turf. It was easy climbing. Eventually she was just below where her bag had disappeared and she saw it, caught in the gorse. Then her eyes widened. Underneath the gorse, cut into the cliff face and invisible from above or either side, was a tiny shelter. A little patch of grass was in front of it. There was even a rock seat.

Abbey pulled down her bag, sat on the seat and leaned back against the rock. There was a perfect view of the castle and the headland. She wondered who had come here first. Might it have been some castle-dweller in the Middle Ages? It was possible. Certainly it didn't seem as if anyone had been here for years. The sun shone down and warmed her.

She would sit here for a while. She felt protected, at peace with the world. This would be a good place to think. So she leaned against the rock, closed her eyes and thought about the first day of her new life. And the day wasn't yet over!

Why did she think first about John Cameron, and not about Scotland or the job? He seemed a pleasant enough man—though there was an edge of danger to him. She had to admit, she was attracted to him. Physically he was superb—but that didn't count for too much. She thought she had detected a sense of fun in him. And there was a gentleness, an easiness about him that she hadn't met in many men recently.

While she'd worked in the hospital she'd been out with a couple of men who'd known something of her background. But nothing had come of it. Either they had been too busy working, or they hadn't been able to cope with her necessarily erratic lifestyle. When they'd parted, she hadn't worried much. Really, she had no time for men.

But now, of course, she did have time. If she was interested. And she had found herself quite interested in John Cameron—and suspected that he might be interested in her.

Rather a lot to decide after one short meeting, she thought.

But she was cautious. She saw something in him that reminded her of her dead husband. It had been when she had watched him looking out to sea, had seen the half-smile on his lips. It had been the face of a man who craved excitement. A man who wanted to know what was over the horizon, a man who would never settle down to a job in one place. She didn't want another man like that.

She was getting ahead of herself. All there was between them so far was the prospect of a drink at her hotel. Still...he was a handsome man.

Perhaps it was time to go back. She climbed up to the clifftop path, knowing she would come to this little eyrie again. Then she walked back to her hotel. Her new life was turning out to be quite exciting.

She showered, washed her hair and changed into trousers and a T-shirt. Then she downloaded the pictures from her camera and sent them with an e-mail to her brother and nieces in Florida. A quick meal in the hotel's dining room and then back to her room to wait until it was time to meet John.

What should she wear? She didn't want to be too formal, and yet she wanted to be feminine. She thought it important to keep her femininity while she was working. The last thing she wanted was to be one of the lads, it just never worked. On the other hand, she didn't want to dress up too much. This was just a casual meeting between two people who might become friends, but who would certainly have to work together.

But she couldn't help feeling just a little bit excited.

In the end she put on a pretty blue cotton dress. She spent some time on her make-up—and thought she looked rather nice. Then she went downstairs, intending to sit in the hotel lounge and read the newspapers until he arrived. But he was already there.

She guessed that he, too, had made a bit of an effort. He was dressed in light grey trousers, a pressed white shirt with a fawn linen jacket. She could see heads were turning to look at him.

He must have positioned himself so he could watch for her arrival. He stood as she came down the stairs.

'I'm not sure you look like a ship's doctor,' he said. 'Far too attractive. Most ship's doctors I've met have been leathery men with very little hair.'

'Give me time. I need to worry more before I get the weather-beaten look. And, in fact, at the moment you don't look too much like a typical diver.'

'As you say, give me time. Shall we go into the bar or would you like to sit on the terrace?'

'It's still warm. I'd like to sit outside.'

So he took her onto a terrace that overlooked the

garden, and ordered her a glass of white wine, while he had a glass of red.

'So will you worry about being a woman on a ship full of men?' he asked.

'Not at all. I'm a professional, I know my job. I can put up with the odd joke, I don't mind that. But I shall tell them that anyone who thinks they can cut corners, ignore my professional judgement—I'll pull their diver's certificate on the spot.'

'You'd do that?'

'Just watch me. I'm as safety-mad as you are.'

'You'll fit in,' he said. 'They're a good bunch of men.' Then he added, in a different tone, 'You're rubbing your finger again, where you used to wear your wedding ring. Do you think about your husband often?'

She was irritated with herself. It was hard to explain that rubbing her finger was just a physical thing, and had nothing to do with memories. 'I think about him very little,' she said shortly. 'It wasn't very successful, it's in the past. I want to live for now, for the present. I hate it when people go on about their past mistakes, how things might have been.'

'You're probably right. Tomorrow is the first day of the rest of your life. I'm going to forget my past, too. If I can.'

She wanted to change the subject. 'Tell me about the ship,' she said. 'I'm looking forward to working on her.'

'Well, starting with the top, and the most important person, you'll get on with the captain. Captain Farrow is ex-Royal Navy and he won't tolerate careless behaviour from anyone. He's a good leader. If you do your job, there's nothing he won't do for you. If you don't do your job, you'll find yourself on the harbour wall.'

'I phoned him after I'd met you. I said I'd drop in to see him tomorrow morning, just for a chat. He said that he'd like to start diving the day after and was there any chance of me working tomorrow afternoon? I said if he needed me, I'd come.'

'Good decision. The captain will appreciate that.'

'He seemed OK to me,' Abbey said. 'Gave me an excuse to back out if I wanted to. But just what exactly are we doing on this trip? I need more details.'

'It's a fairly straightforward job…' John said.

And after that she enjoyed their evening together. Mostly they talked about the job they had to do in the future, both seemed to have accepted that they would not talk about their pasts. An hour slid by and she found herself yawning.

'You're tired,' he said. 'I've kept you out of bed, and you've driven all the way from London.'

She couldn't help herself, she yawned again. 'I've enjoyed our talk, John, but I think you're right. I've enjoyed our chat, but I'll say goodnight now.'

She held out her hand, he shook it. She didn't want to kiss him or be kissed, that might come later. Or not.

'I've enjoyed this evening, too. Goodnight, Abbey.' He hesitated a moment and then said, 'And good luck with your new life.' Then he was gone.

Abbey went to her room, undressed and went straight to bed. For a minute or two she lay awake. She thought she rather liked John. That was all, she rather liked him. But she didn't know him. And there was a reserve about him that had sometimes seemed odd.

Well, time would tell. This was her new life and tomorrow was the first day of it. She was smiling as she went to sleep.

CHAPTER TWO

SHE had told John when she'd arrive at the quayside and there was a sailor waiting for her there with a launch. She had dressed suitably. Trousers—obviously—and a sensible shirt and jacket. Her medical bag was in her hand. She felt smart. And she was looking forward to seeing John again.

The *Hilda Esme* was impressive. She was a converted trawler, but the conversion had been carefully done. And she was neat. Not a rope out of place, no baggage cluttering the decks. Abbey felt she could see the Royal Navy influence.

There was a gangway leading up the side of the ship, and at the top, waiting for her, was John.

He was dressed in engineers' blue overalls, a smudge of oil on one arm. She couldn't help thinking that whatever he wore he looked good in. There was that casual smile—but did she detect just a hint of mischief in it?

He said, 'I'm afraid the captain has been called away unexpectedly to Head Office. He sends his apologies, but the first mate will welcome you. I'll take you to him, he's expecting you.'

Now she was certain. Something was amusing John.

He led her towards the bridge. 'I enjoyed our drink last night,' he said. 'Did you sleep well afterwards?'

'Very well, thank you. John, I'm not sure I like the way you're smiling. What's so funny?'

He looked at her, all innocence. 'Nothing's funny! I'm smiling because I'm glad you're joining the ship.' He opened a door waved her into the bridge. 'May I present our first mate. Larry Kent.'

Abbey looked at Larry and sighed. Now she knew why John had been smiling. She had met Larry before—she had met dozens of Larrys. The hat cocked at a slightly rakish angle, the confident smile. Larry was a ladykiller. And it looked like she had just made him very happy.

He grabbed her hand, held it in both of his. 'Abbey! It's good to meet you. And aren't we lucky to have such a beautiful woman on board?'

She managed to free her hand. 'On board I'm a doctor,' she said. 'And that's how I expect to be treated.'

'Of course. What else? I'm sure you're very competent. But we have to work together, get to know each other. Look, the captain says that he wants to brief you in person. But there's still lots we have to discuss even though the captain's not here, things we have to settle. What about having dinner with me tonight? Before we start work properly?'

Abbey looked sideways, saw John still with the secret smile. Now she knew what had caused it.

'I would have loved to have dinner with you, Larry,' she said, 'but I'm already going out to dinner with John here.'

She saw John stop smiling, look confused.

'You two know each other?' Larry asked, obviously rather upset.

'We've met,' Abbey said. 'Now, if it's all right with you, I'd like John to show me around my surgery and so on.'

'Of course,' said Larry. 'Well, I'm sure we'll see more of each other later.'

Abbey felt pleased with herself.

'You knew what Larry was like, didn't you?' she asked as they walked the length of the ship. 'You knew he'd come on to me. That's why you were smiling. Why didn't you warn me?'

'I knew you'd cope with him. I just wanted to see it.'

'So am I going to have trouble with him?'

'Not you, you're tough. You can handle him. What was that about us having dinner tonight?'

'Well, since it seemed to be a choice between having dinner with you and having dinner with Larry. I chose you. But it was a hard decision.'

'Now, why isn't that a compliment that I feel I can treasure?' he muttered.

He opened a door. 'This is your surgery,' he said.

Abbey walked in, impressed. It was obviously a specialist surgery—there was little there that was connected with disease. Instead it was a place where a kind of top-grade first aid could be given. She had been told at her interview that any serious cases would be sent to hospital. However, no expense had been spared on the equipment that was there.

'Hyperbaric chamber through here.' John opened another door. 'Just a one-man chamber, one of those new American ones, but it's pretty good.'

Abbey looked at the chamber. It looked vaguely ominous, a narrow bed covered with a bubble of transparent plastic, with attached chrome machinery and controls.

'You know how to use it?'

'I've taken the course. If you can maintain it, I can use it.'

'I can maintain it. Now, what more can I show you?'

'Just leave me here to look around,' she said.

Abbey had been appointed as ship's doctor, but with special responsibility for the divers. Captain Farrow was in overall charge of the ship. Larry's responsibility was the crew—the engineers, deckhands, cooks and radio officer. John was in charge of the divers and the diving equipment. The system appeared to work well.

The captain had arranged with John that all the divers should come on board that afternoon and be examined by Abbey. And before they could dive, each of them had to produce his certificate of medical fitness, issued by a health and safety executive approved medical examiner of divers. Abbey was an approved examiner, she was on the HSE list. But the divers all already had them. Abbey had photocopies of the certificates on file and she'd read through them before starting her examinations.

'Do you want me to be present when you see them?'
John asked.

'As a chaperon? For them or for me?' Abbey asked
with a grin. 'Yes, I think it might be a good idea if you
were with me. You're going to be in charge of them
while they're diving, so it's important that you know as
much about their physical states as possible. But you're
not coming into my surgery dressed in overalls.'

'No, ma'am,' he said, and left.

She got on quite well with most of the men. In each
case Abbey started by telling them about her diving
medical qualifications. After that things got easier.

The examination was just the usual things at first—
pulse, heart beat, blood pressure and so on. But there
were certain areas that Abbey looked at with more
than usual attention. Diving produced unique strains
on the body so she looked at capacity for exercise,
how the cardiovascular system and the respiratory
system would react under stress. She paid particular
attention to ear, nose and throat and even to dentition.
Teeth had been known to explode underwater if there
was a sealed cavity and the pressure was great
enough.

After each examination she gave herself five minutes
to chat to each diver, to ask if he had been ill, how much
work he'd had recently. If he had been abroad. It was difficult, but she also had to try to work out if there were
any personal problems that might affect a man's judgement. Professional diving demanded total concentration.

During all of this John stayed in the room but busied

himself checking supplies, writing down orders and so on. But Abbey knew that he was listening

All went reasonably well until Dave Evans came in, the last but one she was due to examine. Abbey treated him just as she had all the others—shook hands, talked about herself, tried to make the man comfortable.

While doing this, she observed. She remembered her old professor telling her that nothing a patient told her should come as a surprise. A good doctor would often have some idea of what was wrong before the patient opened his or her mouth. The body was a book, and she had to learn to read it.

Abbey didn't like what she read in Dave's body. For a start, he was the oldest of the divers. His body mass seemed high, his face was podgy and there was an unhealthy flush to it. And although he tried to hide it, he was having difficulty with his breathing.

She checked. His medical diving certificate was due to run out in five weeks—they only lasted for a year. Casually, she asked, 'Why didn't you get your certificate renewed, Dave? It hasn't got long to go.'

Dave tried to shrug, but Abbey thought there was something rather uncomfortable about his manner. 'Never quite got round to it. I've spent a lot of time with my family.'

'Had any serious illnesses in the past year—any illnesses at all?'

Another shrug. 'Had a couple of colds—but doesn't everybody?'

'It's common,' Abbey agreed. 'Now, take off your shirt and let's start with your blood pressure.'

She was wrapping the cuff round his arm when there was a knock on her door. John went to answer it and she heard a murmured conversation. Then John was by her side.

'There's a consignment of diving supplies been delivered to the dockside, I really ought to check it all before it comes on board. If you don't really…'

'I can manage without you, John,' she said. 'I've nearly finished here. We can talk later.' He left.

She felt rather alone when John had gone. He hadn't contributed much to her examinations but she had been glad of his quiet presence in the room. And now she needed him more than ever.

She didn't like the crackle in Dave's chest. She listened to his heart again, then went back to his lungs.

'Just how bad were these colds you had, Dave? And how long since the last one?'

He didn't like her questions. 'They were just colds! A running nose, a bit of a cough.'

'How long did you have the cough for? You've had it recently, and it lasted more than a few days, didn't it?'

'It was nothing,' Dave said sullenly.

She double-checked her findings, thought for a minute. Then, after Dave had put his shirt back on, she said, 'Bad news, I'm afraid, Dave. You're not fit to dive at present. You won't be fit for at least a week. You've got a chest congestion and in my opinion that makes you—'

'In your opinion! Dr Fraser, I've been diving for twenty years now and I've always been fit. I've given good service. I feel fine now. I've dived when I've felt like this before and there's no reason why I shouldn't dive with the others!'

His tone became more reasonable, coaxing even. 'Let's face it, this isn't much of a dive. Thirty-odd metres, that's shallow water to me. I can handle it easily.'

Abbey sighed. 'There is a reason why you shouldn't dive. Your lungs are half full of mucus. You'd be risking your life and so I'm recommending—'

'You recommend what you like! I'm going to find someone who isn't a jumped-up little girl fresh out of medical school.'

He stormed out of the surgery, slamming the door behind him. Abbey sighed again. She could have done without this.

She had one more examination to make, but she could do with a break. Opening her door, she shouted, 'I'll see the last man in a quarter of an hour.' Then she shut the door before anyone could reply.

She wasn't altogether surprised when there was a knock on her door ten minutes later, but she was surprised to see Larry with Dave. Larry looked uncomfortable. 'If we could just have a word, Abbey?' he said. 'This should really be John Cameron's job but he's on shore and…'

Silently she waved the two men to chairs. 'Before we start,' she said, 'Mr Evans, I can only divulge your medical details to a third person with your permission. Do I have that permission?'

This question upset Dave, he hadn't been expecting it. 'Well, I dunno…' he said. 'Do we have to go into detail?'

'The thing is, Abbey,' Larry broke in, 'not having Dave diving will upset our schedule. The work will suffer. And if he doesn't dive, he only gets standby pay, which isn't very much. He's got family responsibilities, he needs the money. All we're asking for is a little give and take. If he takes things easy, if John gives him diving work that doesn't require too much stress, I'm sure that things will be OK.'

The unfortunate thing was that Larry was partly right. Having Dave dive wouldn't be too much of a risk. But it would be a risk and she wasn't going to take it.

'In my professional opinion, Dave is not fit to dive,' she said. 'If he wishes I will send the results of my examination to another doctor and he can have a second opinion. But at present the only way that Dave can dive is if I get a note signed by the captain saying that he has seen my recommendations and chosen to ignore them. And if I get that note, I'll walk off the ship at once.'

It was difficult for her not to smile when she saw Larry's shocked face. This was not the reaction he had expected from a sweet lady doctor. 'Well, we'll have to see,' he said. 'Come on, Dave.'

'Will you tell the divers that I'd like a word with them all afterwards?' Abbey shouted after him.

They were waiting for her in the divers' messroom. She could feel the hostility the moment she walked in. Well, she had expected it. She wished John was there. She knew he'd be on her side and suspected he'd make her job easier. But she was the doctor and she had made the decision. This was something she had to do.

'You've all heard that I've stopped Dave from diving—at least for a while. Well, I'm sorry, and I've contacted a consultant in Aberdeen to see if we can get him back to work. I didn't set the rules on this, though I do agree with them. Dave didn't meet a certain medical standard that the HSE thinks is necessary. So he doesn't dive.'

She paused, took a breath. 'I'm going to mention one thing and then I don't want it ever brought up again. And I'm not looking for sympathy. My husband was a diver and he died because he didn't stick to the rules. And more than that, perhaps he died because his buddy let him get away with not sticking to the rules. You're responsible for each other. A sick man can't even look after himself, never mind his buddy.'

She could tell she had their attention now. The hostility had waned, and even Dave looked less angry.

'So let me remind you of the rules. I want to know of any illness—any suggestion of an illness—well before it develops. I want to know of any cut, scratch, bruise or toothache, no matter how small. If it's nothing—which it will be most of the time—then I'll tell you. But I make the decisions.

'And remember! Don't drink to excess before diving. And that means tonight. If I think you're under the influence, I'll test you and I'll stop you. One thing I stand by. I suppose everyone's got the right to be stupid and risk their own life. But no one's got the right to risk the life of his buddy. OK?'

One more point to make. 'Last thing, I'm a diver my-self—though definitely an amateur. In fact, I've got the PADI master scuba diving rating. And, believe it or not, I like divers. Thank for listening.'

She thought she'd got her message across. The PADI rating—the Professional Association of Diving Instructors—was the highest amateur qualification there was. It was respected. The men were looking at each other, nodding, whispering, and seemed a bit more re-laxed. She kept her face bland. Quietly, she sighed with relief.

She waited for John in the lounge of the hotel that eve-ning. This time she was wearing a rose-coloured dress. Soon she would be running out of pretty clothes. She had packed mostly for a working six or eight weeks— trousers, shirts, sweaters and plenty of outdoor gear. It had been all she had expected to need. And she also hadn't really expected to meet someone like John.

So she sat there and tried to work out how she felt. Workwise, she felt things weren't going too badly. With any luck, she'd get on with the divers. She was quite looking forward to the next day when they would put out to sea.

So that was half of her new life. How did she feel about John? Perhaps the other half of her new life?

She just didn't know. Physically, he was certainly one of the most attractive men she had ever met. But she needed more than that. Her husband had been a fine specimen of a man—might John have the same faults as him? Just what else did she need in a man? What was she looking for? She didn't know. But it might be quite fun finding out.

He walked into the lounge at that moment, and, whatever she was thinking, there was no doubt about what she was feeling. This couldn't be. She was too experienced to feel simple lust! But certainly she caught her breath, felt a warmness in her cheeks, a reaction in her body that left her almost lost for words. She hadn't felt this way in years!

'Every time I see you, you're dressed differently and you always look so attractive,' he said.

'Thank you, kind sir. Even in my medical outfit this morning?'

'Especially in that outfit.'

'Well, you look quite smart yourself,' she said.

And he did. Perhaps he, too, was coming to the end of his wardrobe, but that evening he was wearing a dark blue linen suit with a light blue silk shirt. Very smart indeed. The suit matched his dark blue eyes, and she wondered if he had picked it on purpose. She noticed his eyes were fixed on her with an intensity that hadn't been there before. Perhaps he was feeling the same way as she was. Oh, dear!

But his manner was calm as he escorted her out to his car. 'I thought we might drive out of Dunlort,' he said. 'There's a very pleasant restaurant just off the main road. And Dunlort is a small place, there's just a chance that Larry might turn up—by accident, of course. He's fond of a drink.'

'I'm not going to cause trouble between you and him, am I? I don't want that.'

John shook his head. 'On board Larry is perfectly responsible, a good first mate. The captain wouldn't have anything else.'

'Good. On board I want to concentrate on work, not have to bother with any man-woman nonsense.'

'Sounds a good plan,' he said, and she decided the subject was closed.

She stared out of the window at the green hills and the blue sky, felt the warmth of the sun through the windscreen. 'John, isn't it a perfect evening?'

'It is. Before I came here I was working in the Gulf. The sun there was just too much. I used to lie in my bunk and dream of being out in the rain.'

'This is Scotland. Your dream is likely to come true quite soon.'

'I'm sure my dream will come true,' he said softly, and she wondered what he meant.

It was a pleasant restaurant and they were given a table on the verandah. She supposed the food was good but she didn't pay too much attention to it. The wine might have been good, too, but she only had two glasses, and noticed once again that John only had one glass. But she wasn't there just to eat. She wanted to talk to John.

'What was working in the Gulf like?' she asked.

He shrugged. 'Hard and hot. But the work was quite interesting. I was helping to fix oil pipes underwater. And the money was very good.'

'So where next?'

That shrug again. 'Wherever takes my fancy. There's always work for a skilled diver. I might go back to the Gulf, I might go to the Caribbean, there's a lot of work in Australia. Or I might just wander for a while.'

'And you're usually well paid?'

This question seemed to interest him, as if he hadn't thought about it before. 'I suppose I am. I don't think much about it. If the money's there, good. If not, well, I'll always cope.'

'So you're not saving for your home somewhere? Or for your family?'

That seemed to amuse him and he laughed. 'I've got no family and never had a home. I was an orphan, brought up in an orphanage. I suppose I was well looked after, I never felt I was missing anything. Then I joined the navy. I did a few years there and loved the life. And since I left I go wherever my fancy takes me.'

'No permanent relationships, then?' Abbey asked cautiously.

He laughed again. 'You mean relationships with a woman? Never a permanent one. I've had girlfriends, of course, but I like being a wanderer, a loner. And most women don't understand that.'

'Quite,' said Abbey. 'You mean you have no family at all?'

'No family at all. And I'm not sorry. Families always seem to drag you down. When this job is finished I'll go where I want, consult no one. I'm free. Have you got a family, Abbey?'

'A brother in Florida and two nieces I dote on.'

It surprised her that she was finding John so easy to talk to. He appeared interested but relaxed, and she felt she could confide in him. And she wanted him to know a little about her.

She went on, 'My family is everything to me. My father died six weeks ago, and it changed my life. I've spent the last three years looking after him. He had chronic lymphocytic leukemia, and it grew progressively worse. We knew there was no hope but we were together and that was great. Lots of times he told me I should leave him, that he could manage in a nursing home and I should go and get a life. But I loved him and I wanted to stay with him.'

She couldn't help it. A tear ran down her cheek. She scrabbled in her bag for a tissue but before she could find one John passed her his handkerchief.

'You loved him,' John said quietly. 'Now you're feeling the pain of his death. Was the love worth the pain?'

'Yes, it was! My mother died when I was eleven, my father brought me up. Watching him die did hurt, but I thought of what we'd had before and it was plenty. Love's like nothing else. The more you give, the more you get.'

'An interesting thought. You don't think that the more you love, the more you leave yourself open to pain?'

'There is that,' she said. She wondered where this conversation was going. John wasn't being argumentative, trying to make a point. He seemed genuinely interested in what she thought.

'You haven't mentioned your husband,' he said.

'And I'm not going to. My marriage was a mess. I had hopes, I did work at it, but I'd made a stupid mistake. In fact, we'd both made a stupid mistake. But now I've moved on, I'm free of the memories. I'm not looking back.'

She was glad when he accepted the hint and said no more.

She enjoyed her meal. The restaurant was pleasant, the food was good, but she was enjoying herself because she was with John. When they had finished it was still light. They decided not to stay too long over coffee but to drive back to Dunlort.

'We're going to be mostly working at sea from now on,' she said. 'I'd like to walk a bit on dry land first.'

'Suits me. And it's still a gorgeous evening.'

So they drove back to Dunlort and she took him walking along the clifftop path. When they came within sight of the castle she got him to scramble down after her, and they sat together in her little eyrie. He was as entranced as she had been. 'How did you find this place? There's no sign of it from above.'

'Just chance,' she said. 'Sometimes you get lucky.'

They sat side by side on the rock seat and gazed out to sea, both, for the moment, quite content to be silent. The sun was now setting, turning the blue sea to gold. He put his arm around her shoulders, and after a moment's hesitation she leaned against him and slipped an arm round his waist.

It had been so long since she'd done anything like

this. There had been a couple of odd meetings with colleagues she had met at the hospital, but they had been rushed affairs, and ultimately unsatisfactory. Her father and her work had come first. But now she was free. And sitting here with John was almost like being seventeen again, and out on her first serious date.

His arm slid further round her shoulders and he gently pulled her towards him. She could feel how tentative he was, knew that she could stop this at any moment. But, really, she didn't want to.

She closed her eyes, lifted her face up to him—and he kissed her.

She had forgotten what it was like to be kissed—or had she ever been kissed like this before? Her head was reeling. She was conscious of nothing but the strength of his arms around her, the softness of his mouth as he teased hers. Without thinking she parted her lips, moaned softly as their kiss deepened. His arms tightened, she felt her breasts respond almost painfully, hinting at a need that she had ignored for too long.

Then he stopped kissing her. She was disappointed. He eased away from her and she opened her eyes to see his face, still close. She couldn't read his expression. Certainly there was desire there—he had wanted her as much as she had wanted him. But there was something else. He looked…baffled?

'You don't have to stop kissing me,' she said. 'I'm not objecting.'

'I don't want to stop. Lord knows, I don't want to stop. But…but I like you, Abbey, and I want to be fair to you.'

'Go on, then. Be fair. But I thought it was usually women who had doubts at this stage.'

'Possibly so. But I want to get things straight between us. First, I like women. But I've never deceived one. I'm not a good risk, I'm a loner. There's going to be no future in any relationship with me.'

She looked at him sardonically. 'Usually when a man says that, he thinks that it absolves him of all later blame. He says don't fall in love with me, this is all at your risk, but he does nothing to stop the woman falling for him. John, that's just not fair.'

He sighed and the arm that had been round her waist fell away. 'I've never wanted to cause anyone pain,' he said.

'Fine. I'll ensure that you don't cause me pain. I'll give you a guarantee. And now you can kiss me again. If you want to.'

'I do! But…we'll be working together. Is this a good idea?'

'Probably not,' she said. 'But for once I don't care. I'm starting a new life, perhaps I'm entitled to make a few mistakes.'

So he kissed her again and it was even better than before. Abbey wondered—then she stopped wondering and just enjoyed. For the moment there was no future, just the present.

He stopped kissing her—again. And again she was disappointed. 'I want to carry on kissing you,' he said.

'Good. I feel the same way myself.' She saw the same expression on his face, as if he was puzzled, baffled even, not sure of what was happening. Surely it was obvious? 'Is anything wrong?' she asked.

He moved even further from her and frowned. Then he reached forward, took her hand in his, pressed it to his chest. 'Can you feel my heart beat?'

'I'm a doctor, I'm good at heartbeats. And I can feel yours without a stethoscope. It's fast.'

'You're the reason why. I've got an odd feeling that I'm being given something and it's not something that I want to treat lightly. It might be something precious.' He paused a moment and then added, 'And this feeling is new to me.'

Now it was Abbey's turn to feel cautious. What John had just said was too much like a declaration. She needed to be more certain about things. She stood, reached and pulled him upright. Then she leaned forward and quickly kissed him on the cheek.

'Perhaps we'd better go back now. We'll have a lot of time together over the next few weeks so there's no need to rush anything. Heavens, it was only yesterday that I met you for the first time.'

'True.' He looked out to sea. The sun had now disappeared and the sea was darkening. 'I've never met anyone quite like you, Abbey. I don't know how to deal with it.'

'You'll find a way,' she said.

They walked back along the clifftop to her hotel in companionable silence. When they got there he offered to carry any of her heavy baggage down to the harbour so she invited him to her room to pick it up.

As she packed a few things he alooked round the

room, studied the photographs she had put out. 'You're only here for two nights and yet you've turned this into a little home,' he said.

'I like photographs. There's my dad, that's my brother and the nieces, that group are the people I worked with at the hospital.'

'No pictures of your husband?'

'I told you, that's over. I'm forgetting him. Now, if you can take this trunk down, I'd be pleased.'

'No trouble.' She had struggled to get the trunk upstairs, but he picked it up casually and threw it over his shoulder.

They went down to his car. It was now dusk. She kissed him quickly on the lips but like a friend, not a lover. 'See you tomorrow,' she said. Then she was gone, without a backward glance.

Once back in her room she showered and then went straight to bed. She was not going to think about anything, not examine what she had done, consider how she was feeling. For a while she was content just to be. And she had enjoyed the evening more than any she'd had in months.

There was sleeping accommodation, cabins, a galley and so on aboard the *Hilda Esme*. But the salvage company had decided that the ship should come back into port at night. The dive site was only about ten miles away and if they were only at sea in daylight then they would need a much smaller crew. So the diving section was billeted in a hostel on the dockside which belonged to a university that ran marine biology courses. The McElvey Centre was comfortable. Each diver had his own *en suite* room, there was a dining hall with a very good cook and recreational facilities in a lounge. There was even a small sick bay.

The divers were happy with this arrangement. So was John, though he kept a careful eye open to make sure none of them drank too much. But it wasn't likely to happen.

John took the trunk to the slightly larger cabin next to the sick bay, which had been allocated to Abbey. Then he went back to his own cabin.

As he looked around he realised that there wasn't a single item of decoration there. There was a work schedule, a couple of charts, a diagram of the ship they were to dive on. He'd been there a week already but it was far less a home than Abbey's hotel room. For the first time in his life he wondered if he was missing something. Or was there something missing in him? The two questions were different.

He kicked off his shoes and lay on his bed, his hands behind his head. And he thought about Abbey.

First of all he thought about how she looked. He remembered how he had first seen her—a lithe figure in a dark swimming costume. She had dived, her legs in the air, then disappeared. That's when he had wondered if she had been in difficulties.

Then they had swum to the beach together. Not every woman looked at her best in a swimming costume, when her hair was wet through. But Abbey had struck him at once as being absolutely gorgeous.

She was tall, her shoulders perhaps a tiny touch broader than was fashionable. Who cared about fashion? Her body was slim and there were curves to arms and legs that showed how she exercised regularly. Funny, he couldn't quite tell what it was that attracted him about her face. But it was lovely. Eyes, lips, teeth, short dark hair—all were fine. But together they formed a whole that echoed her personality. She was direct, interested and interesting. He couldn't imagine tiring of looking at her, listening to her.

He wondered if he was changing. For the first time in his life he was vaguely wondering what it would be like to share his life with someone. Settle down! A house in one place, a mortgage, the same job every morning? That just wasn't him, the very thought of it made him cringe.

But if he did settle down, someone like Abbey would be the person he'd like to settle down with.

He thought of her delight in her nieces. If Abbey settled down, she'd certainly want children. Children were a danger. He remembered his own childhood, as he wouldn't want to inflict that on anyone.

He jumped off the bed. poured himself a glass of water. And another thing. A full-time long-term relationship was not an easy thing to start. And he was not as confident as he'd once been. He knew he was harsher on the men than was strictly necessary. He just didn't want to take risks. So how could he begin a relationship when he felt himself a failure?

CHAPTER THREE

A VERY early start next morning. Abbey had to move the rest of her bags to the McElvey Centre then report for duty. She was half excited, half apprehensive. This was going to be something new for her.

There was the usual doctor's white coat for her on board, but for now she dressed in sensible trousers and sweater. This wasn't like the first day in a hospital, where she'd wear a formal suit. This was a different form of medicine—and she was looking forward to it.

Perhaps John had been waiting for her because the minute she parked her car outside the centre, he was standing by the door.

He was dressed in thick jeans and a dark T-shirt, a sweater knotted around his neck. He looked tall and fit and virile and she felt a tremor of excitement run through her. This was the man who had kissed her last night, and…today she was here to work!

'I'll carry your things to your room and then we'll get on board,' he said.

He looked at the sea, the sky, the ship. 'It's going to be a good day for diving,' he added.

Only a few words but Abbey recognised the tone of voice. She had heard it before in other men. A longing to find out what was over the horizon. A determination never to settle. In its way it was a bit frightening.

'We'd better get started, then,' she said. 'All the men OK?'

'All fine. Dave Evans is being driven to the hospital in Aberdeen this morning. The men like it that you've moved so quickly for him. You seem to have got them on your side.'

'I like them. But I'm going to do no one any favours.'

'I think they know that,' John said.

She nodded and smiled at the divers as they walked along the quay and climbed into the launch that took them out to the ship. Once on board she was escorted to the captain's cabin, told that he would be in to see her the minute they had cleared the harbour.

And then they set off. There were all the exciting noises—the rattle of the chains as they left their mooring buoys, the rumble of the engines changing in tone as they gathered way. She could feel the vibration of the engines, feel the gentle movement of the deck as the ship cleared the harbour mouth and headed out to sea. Perhaps she could feel a little of the excitement that John felt. It felt good to be alive.

'Dr Fraser, good to meet you. I'm Captain Caleb Farrow.' She turned, there in the cabin door was a short, broad figure. He was white-haired, white-bearded, but there was an air of decisiveness about him that gave him authority. It was a lot to decide on a first impression, but Abbey suspected that she was going to be happy working for this man.

'Pleased, to meet you, too, Captain,' she said, holding out her hand. 'I'm happy to be on board.'

'Good, good. Sit down and we'll talk a little.' He took off his cap, laid it carefully on the table. The two of them sat facing each other, and she discovered he had the most piercing blue eyes. Captain Caleb Farrow was quite something.

'When I joined the Royal Navy,' he said, 'in those days there were no women on board ship. Like all the other sailors, I thought that having females in the crew on board would ruin discipline and turn a crew into a rabble. I was wrong. Later on, many of my most efficient crew members were female. I think ships were better because of them. So you are welcome on board. Now, your duties.'

Abbey managed not to smile. The captain had put her at her ease—now they could start work. Well, she did feel at ease with him.

'The first thing is, I'm captain. If there's anything you think I ought to know, I want to know it. Medical confidentiality doesn't work the same way on board ship.'

Abbey thought for a moment. 'Tell just you? No one else on board?'

'Just me.'

She thought a little more. 'If I think anyone's medical condition might endanger the ship, endanger the man's life or endanger the life on anyone on board, and I couldn't persuade him to take the obvious actions, then I'll tell you, permission or no permission.'

'I'll settle for that. You know the conditions that might be dangerous?'

'I have studied diving medicine,' she said. 'I have certificates to prove it.'

'Of course. Just one last thing. I have every confidence in John Cameron. He's a good man, he'll look after his men. But the divers are working to a deadline. If they get the work finished early then there will be a very substantial bonus for them. It's possible that some of them might be tempted to cut corners, say, to dive when they have some kind of slight respiratory condition. I want you to see that doesn't happen. And, Doctor, whatever your decision, I will back you up.'

'I'll see everyone is safe to dive,' she said. 'And thanks for your confidence in me.'

The captain smiled. 'I've got a son who's studying medicine in Edinburgh,' he said. 'He's in his last year. I like doctors.' Then he stood. Her interview was over.

She felt happy as she left his cabin. With a leader like Captain Farrow, this would be a good ship to work on.

First she went to her surgery and once again checked that she knew where everything was. John was talking to the divers. She knew he had already briefed them on what they were going to be doing that day, but it wouldn't hurt to run over things a second time.

After a while there was nothing to do so she went on deck, smelt the sea air, rejoiced in the ship's thrust as it bounced through the waves. And when someone came and leaned on the rail next to her, she knew who it would be. It was John.

His arm slid along the rail, touched hers. Accident or design?

'You're smiling,' he said. 'Are you so pleased to be starting work?'

'Well, you are pleased,' she pointed out. 'Why not me? No, it's always the same when you put out to sea. There's that feeling of excitement, of there being something new coming up.'

He nodded. 'I feel it, too. But no matter how exciting it is at first, after a while the job gets a bit same-ish. Then you start to wonder what is over the next horizon.'

'Always?'

He paused before answering. 'For me, so far it's been always.' There was another pause, and she turned to look at him. He was staring out to sea, as if the answer to some question was there. And when he spoke he didn't turn to look at her. 'Last night,' he said, 'in your eyrie, I want to say that I really…really enjoyed it. It was…something to me.'

'It was something to me, too,' she said honestly.

'But afterwards I felt a bit…a bit frightened.'

'I don't think I've ever frightened a man before by kissing him. What were you frightened of? Me?'

'I think I was frightened of new horizons,' he said. 'Do you know what I'm talking about? Because I don't.'

She knew she had to answer carefully but she

didn't know what to say. 'I think that perhaps you and me have—'

'John! Want to get the platform ready? We'll be there in fifteen minutes.'

She turned and there was one of the divers, looking impatient. She glanced at John. For a moment he seemed not to have understood the question. But then he hunched his shoulders and forced his attention to the question.

'We can start,' he said, 'but there's a couple of checks I need to go through first. See you later, Abbey.'

She was dismissed, he had work to do. Well, fair enough. But she wondered where their conversation had been going.

She could see their destination now, a large flat-looking ship, like an ocean-going barge. It wasn't moving but was moored at stem and stern. Amidships there was a crane.

'This is a manoeuvre I've done a thousand times,' a voice said. 'But young Kent hasn't and he needs the practice. So I'm going to chat to you and hope he can manage.'

Abbey turned and smiled at Captain Farrow. 'If he gets anything wrong you'll be on that bridge in a minute,' she said. 'But if you've got a minute I'd like to know exactly what we're doing here.'

The captain sniffed. 'We're picking up the pieces after someone else's bad seamanship,' he said. 'A hundred feet below us is the wreck of the *Sally J. Crooks*. She was ferrying drums of a particularly expensive oil from Aberdeen to one of the German ports. There was a storm and a collision with one of those scruffy little freighters that are registered in one foreign country, owned in another and crewed by all sorts of half-trained people from a third. The *Sally J. Crooks* sank—fortunately with no loss of life. The freighter sailed off into the night, all sorts of international maritime lawyers are trying to find who owns her and how to sue them.'

'You seem to feel strongly about it, Captain.'

'I do. For a start, if that oil escapes into the sea then the pollution around here will be catastrophic.'

'Which is why we're diving?'

'Exactly.' The captain pointed at the large barge, which was now much nearer. 'Our divers will go down in threes, try to drag and manhandle the oil drums out of the hold so they can be attached to the line of that crane. The crane will lift them aboard the barge, and when the barge is full it will transport them to port.'

'Has any of the oil spilt?'

'Some. The divers will be working in a confined space, in an oil-contaminated environment, so they can hardly see. And there are a lot of metal spikes and rough edges. That's why we need you.'

'They earn their money,' Abbey said, shivering.

'They do.'

But now the captain was looking elsewhere. The *Hilda Esme* had slowed amd was approaching the first of two large buoys. 'Like the barge there, we have permanent moorings at bow and stern,' the Captain muttered. 'Sometimes it's a job picking them up. But young Kent is doing well.'

The ship slowed, her bows slewed round until she nudged the first buoy. Abbey watched as a crew attached the *Hilda Esme* to the buoy and then ran aft to secure her to the second buoy. She was now lying parallel to the barge.

The captain sighed with satisfaction. 'Now it's the divers' turn,' he said. 'I can go and have a coffee.' And he left her.

Abbey had seen operations like this before, but they still fascinated her. She watched as John supervised the launching of the diving platform—a large rubber boat that would be lashed to the side of the ship. Three fully kitted divers climbed clumsily down the ladder to the platform. John followed them. A last check of their kit and the divers fell backwards over the side of the platform, each of them towing a wireless line behind him. Quite near the platform was another, smaller buoy. Abbey knew that below it was a shotline, a guide going down to the wreck below. And close by was the line of the crane on the barge.

After that there wasn't much to see. But she stayed on deck and watched. John had earphones on his head, in constant communication with his divers below. After a while she saw movements by the crane on the barge. And then she heard the noise of the crane's engine and after a while a cage broke the surface of the water, carrying four oil drums. They were swung aboard, presumably stacked safely and the cage lowered underwater again.

She had nothing else to do so she carried on watching. After a while another three divers climbed down the ladder and were briefed by John. Then three heads broke the surface, the three divers who had been below. John helped them over the side of the platform, and the others dived. It seemed a well-organised operation.

Time for Abbey to start work. She was there when the first three divers climbed up the ladder. They seemed happy enough. She'd give then time to get unsuited, have a shower and then she'd have a word with each one. It was probably not really necessary. If they needed her, they'd ask. But she liked to keep an eye on things.

No one did seem to need her. But when the third group had surfaced, changed and had a quick chat with her, she noticed that one of them was limping.

'Harry! What's wrong with the foot?'

He smiled at her uncertainly. 'It's nothing, Doc. No need to worry.'

'Worrying is what I do best. Now, don't argue. Come to the surgery. I want a quick look.'

He had complete articulation so she was pretty sure that no bone was broken. But there was a dark bruise forming on his instep, which must have been painful.

'I'll put a cold compress on this,' she said. 'That should get rid of any swelling and might help the pain. Now, tell me what happened.'

'Moving one of the drums,' Harry mumbled. 'It slipped and my foot was under it.'

'Well, I'm not stopping you diving,' Abbey said. 'Though you might be in some discomfort. But, Harry, in future I want to know! Any accident, no matter how small. And pass the word around.'

'Right,' said Harry.

She had enjoyed her day. When they were heading back to Dunlort she said to John, 'You bought me dinner last night. Could I at least buy you a drink tonight?'

He sighed and then laughed. 'Abbey, I can think of nothing that I would rather do,' he said. 'But I decided to work this evening on the hyperbaric chamber. It probably doesn't need any maintenance, but if I've done it then I know it's been done right. But I'd rather be with you.'

She liked him for that. 'Would you like me to stay and keep you company?'

'I'd love you to. But if you did, would I get much work done?'

'There'll be other nights,' she said.

She had a very good evening meal with the divers at the McElvey Centre, then she went to her room. She had spread her pictures out again. She smiled at them and then sent an e-mail to Florida. But then she felt at a loss. So she thought about John Cameron.

She had only known him—goodness, only three days! And yet that evening she felt his absence. She was tired but she didn't quite know what to do with herself. For a while she even considered sending for the launch and going to see him, whether he wanted her to or not. But then she decided she was being foolish. She would go for a walk instead.

It was inevitable that she should go along the cliff path to her eyrie. Once there she leaned back, looked out towards the harbour. She could just see the *Hilda Esme*, the ship with John on it.

And she thought not about John but about herself.

She had intended starting a new life and she was getting one. She wondered if it was all a bit too soon. She knew that she was—or was capable of being—a passionate woman. But for three years now she had been celibate. Certainly there had been offers, chances, but no one had really tempted her.

She had to admit, she was tempted now. Her body was telling her that she was a young woman, that she had urges, needs, desires, as much as any other healthy young woman.

Not that just satisfying simple physical desire would be enough for her. She must feel for—all right, she must love—the man in question. Could John be such a man? She wasn't sure. Possibly it was just her body that was rebelling, persuading her that John was the man of her dreams. But he was. There was so much more to him than his body.

Abbey stood up, smiled to herself. She felt she had made a decision of some sort. Exactly what that decision was, she wasn't sure.

It was dusk when she walked down the Dunlort main street and she glanced inside the hotel where she had first stayed. She thought she might have a drink before she went to bed. A tiny celebration of her first real day at work.

She could see a handful of people at the bar—and one of them was Larry. At first she decided to walk on—then she asked herself why he should frighten her away.

She walked into the bar and sat next to Larry.

'Expecting anyone, Larry? I don't want to cramp your style.'

He looked at her, as if unable to believe his luck. 'Abbey! No, I'm on my own. But aren't you with John Cameron?'

'He's got work to do on board.'

'His bad luck is my good luck. Now, what'll you have to drink? The red wine here is excellent. We could share a bottle and—'

She held up her hand. 'Larry, I'm just sitting here for ten minutes with a colleague. You. And I'm going to buy my own drink.'

'But I've got to—'

'You've got to do nothing. If you're going to make a big production of it, I'll go now.'

'Don't do that,' he said. 'And I do recommend the red wine.'

And after that they got on quite well. He wasn't too bad a companion and he had some interesting ideas, especially about training seamen. So she stayed a little longer than she had intended.

She waited until he had ordered himself another drink and then stood and said she was going. No, she very definitely didn't need or want him to escort her. Then she walked down to the McElvey Centre and went to bed.

* * *

John had stayed on board overnight. She met him first when she stepped off the launch next morning and climbed aboard.

She asked him about the hyperbaric chamber. It was fine. Then she said, 'I had a drink with Larry Kent last night. I met him by accident, stayed with him for a few minutes. I'm telling you because I don't want to keep anything from you.'

He smiled. 'Once upon a time, if a girl had told me that she'd had a drink with another man, I would have said that she was a free agent. It was her choice, I'd do the same. But I think I feel different about you, Abbey. Somehow.'

'Thank you for that expression of passion,' she said with a grin. 'Incidentally, I went to my eyrie to sit and think. I could just see the boat and I thought of you.'

It was his turn to grin. 'I thought of you, too. When I wasn't thinking about hyperbaric chambers.'

'Yet more unbridled passion,' she said.

CHAPTER FOUR

THE weather was much calmer that day. The ship made good time getting to the moorings and the divers quickly submerged. And it was a successful day's work underwater. The divers were far ahead of schedule, sending up more drums than had been expected.

Each diver was allowed a set amount of time underwater. John had calculated the time according to normal rules. And not all of the time underwater was spent working. The men had to ascend slowly, to make sure bubbles of nitrogen didn't form in their bloodstreams. John had allocated time of ascent, too.

By mid-afternoon all the divers had used up their allocations of time, though a few of them saw no good reason why they should not go down again.

'We'll never have such good conditions again, John,' one of them said. 'And you know that we'd be perfectly safe diving again. Those time limits were drawn up for amateurs and people who are unfit. We're all ready to go. And we'd like the bonus.'

'No,' John said flatly. 'There are rules and while I'm

dive master, we don't break them. Sorry, lads, but diving's over for the day.'

Abbey was interested to notice that no one tried really hard to argue with John. He must have established that he was in charge and that he couldn't be persuaded to mess with the rules. She admired him for this.

He came over to her and said, 'We're not going back to harbour for an hour or so, so I think I'll dive down and see how the work is coming along. I've missed a couple of days.'

'I'll come with you,' she said.

'No, Abbey. You may be a good amateur, but this is professional diving. It's a different game altogether.'

'I don't regard it as a game. I've dived deeper than here, and on wrecks and in much worse conditions than this. I've got my logbook in the surgery—you can look if you like and see what I've done. I'm not quite as experienced as you professionals but I'm by no means an amateur. Incidentally, you shouldn't dive without a buddy.'

Perhaps it was that that convinced him. 'Just so long as you follow me, do what I tell you to and—'

'May it never come true, but one day I might need to dive to give medical aid. I need to know what's what.'

'OK, I guess you're coming,' he said, his voice resigned. 'I saw you'd brought your dry suit on board. Just one thing. Outside the wreck only. You do not try to get inside. It's still far too dangerous. I've got to get into the hold for a quick inspection, but you wait outside the hull.'

'Fair enough,' she said.

She liked diving, and she liked diving even more with John. There was a strange kind of intimacy underwater. They were two silent figures, upside down in a weightless world.

She saw the wreck. First a darker shadow, then she could make out the lines of the ship. It seemed eerie, ghost-like, lying partly on its side on the sea bottom. Then she could see where the collision had occurred, see where the divers had to slide in to get at the oil drums. They were certainly earning their money!

John swam towards the opening in the hold. A specialist firm of divers had come down a fortnight ago and cut an entry hole in the deck. It was big enough for the divers to enter and for them to pull out the drums of oil. But it didn't look welcoming.

John signed for her to hang onto a railing, and she nodded to show that she understood. Then he dived into the hold.

She felt lonely without him. She was an interloper in this world, it belonged to the fish. She looked around, saw nothing but greyness, looked up and saw the silver of her air bubbles trailing towards the surface. What was John doing? How long would he be?

Then slowly he rose through the hole in the deck and held out his hand, forefinger and thumb curled into a circle. All was well. She remembered how she had given him the same sign when they had first met. In the water.

He beckoned her to follow him and they swam around the wreck. He pointed out what was interesting.

He put his arm around her waist and they swam together, side by side, hip to hip.

Then they set off for the surface again, following the shotline. They were face to face, kicking gently—it wasn't safe to rise too fast. She looked at him, tried to read the expression behind the mask over his eyes. No way of doing it.

He indicated that they had to have one of their compulsory stops. She put one hand on his shoulder, pulled him closer to her. Then she took out her mouthpiece, signalled for him to do the same. He did. And she kissed him.

It was more an expression of intent than any indication of love. Their masks were in the way, they had to keep their lips closed. But, under fifty or so feet of water, they kissed each other. He took both her hands, squeezed them. Then they eased apart, each feeling for the mouthpiece, blowing into it to clear it, and then breathing easily as before. It wasn't a difficult thing to do. Training divers were taught what to do if their mouthpiece came out.

Lazily, they swam for the surface. Then they tumbled over the rubber side of the diving platform, took out mouthpieces again and pulled off their fins.

'I've never been kissed underwater before,' he said. 'All sorts of other exciting things have happened to me, but I've never been kissed.'

'Did you like it?'

'Well, yes,' he said. 'Very much so. Why did you kiss me?'

'I was wondering that myself. I just thought I'd like to.'

'It's going to be hard if we have to go for a dive every time we need a little privacy,' he said.

There was more he had to do on board that night. For a start, he supervised the refilling of the air cylinders. Abbey might have wondered about this, but she had seen dive masters at work before. She knew that there was a vast amount of work—preparation, planning, maintenance—that had to be seen to if divers were to be safe.

'I'm sorry,' he said just before she set off for shore on the launch. 'But this just has to be done.'

'I'd be lying if I said I didn't mind,' she said. 'But I understand. And there'll be other evenings. I'll just stay in my room and e-mail my brother and nieces.'

So that was what she did. But she missed him. And when she had finished her e-mail, she thought of how few days she had known John Cameron. But now he seemed to be central to her life. Of course, that was partly because they were working together.

She decided she wasn't in love with him. But he interested her, attracted her. And she thought he felt the same way about her.

The next day was colder, there was a brisk wind and the water was choppy. But conditions were good enough for diving, and the first party went down. Soon there was a message to John on the surface, and she heard the barge's crane whirr into life, then watched as the first set of drums was hoisted out of the water.

Abbey shivered, decided to fetch her coat. John had promised her that he would not be working on board that night so they could go for dinner, or a walk, or a companionable drink. She smiled, she was looking forward to it. Nothing much was going to happen before then, she thought. Just another day. She could not have been more wrong.

It happened just after the second team had dived while Abbey was chatting to the three who had just come up. She liked to have a few words with the divers, just to check that there was no obvious signs of anything wrong.

There a shout, John's voice, calm, though obviously disturbed. 'Abbey, get here now! Accident below!'

She rushed to where he was standing, listening intently on his earphones. She heard him say, 'I'm handing you over to the doctor now. Do exactly what she tells you.' He pulled off the earphones and microphone, handed the set to her.

The voice that spoke to her was calm—divers were trained to remain calm whatever happened underwater. But she thought she could hear anxiety in the man's voice.

'It's Harry, Doc. He snagged the leg of his suit on a piece of steel. It's cut right through the suit and there's blood everywhere. I think…I think it's pulsing out.'

'Whereabouts on the leg?'

'High on the inside of the thigh.'

Abbey winced. It sounded like the femoral artery was cut. 'Are you out of the hold yet?'

'Yes. We want to know what to do.'

Abbey thought she could hear just a touch of panic in the voice. Time for her to be firm, reassuring. 'You can deal with it. I'll tell you how. Have you got any string handy—or wire, or anything like that? About two feet long?'

'There's the lanyard on my knife.'

'Can you use it to put a tourniquet between the cut and the top of his leg?'

She had to remember that this man was trying to perform a difficult first-aid manoeuvre under thirty metres of water, with limited visibility and on a man wearing a thick wetsuit.

'I can try.' For a while, the only sound was of his heavy breathing. Eventually he said, 'Done it. The bleeding has slowed a bit but it hasn't stopped.'

'It won't. Right. Now set off for the surface. Make sure Harry does nothing. You two are to bring him up— but gently. Don't make any of your usual stops as you come up. He hasn't lost consciousness?'

'No. We're moving him now.'

Suddenly she was aware that she was at the centre of a group. Divers and crew members had heard John's shout, had come and clustered round her.

'Shall we suit up, get down and help?' a voice asked.

'No, they'll be here before you can do any good. I want two of you, no more, down there on the platform to help them over the side. Get them new air cylinders, two of them are going straight back below to do their pressure equalisation stops. John, I'll want a giving set and a dressing for his wound. I don't want him climbing the ladder—can you organise a stretcher so we can lift him aboard?'

'No problem.' He looked uneasily at the sky. 'Do we need a chopper? It's not good helicopter weather.'

'I hope not. Let's look at him first. But I suspect the sooner we get him to port, the better.'

She climbed down the ladder to the diving platform, now heaving up and down, slapping against the side of the ship. The weather was getting worse. That was all they needed.

Two dark helmets broke the surface of the sea, then a third. One man was pushed to the front, two divers leaned over the side of the platform and heaved him on board. It only took a minute to unfasten his gear and he was laid on his back in the inches of water that always flooded the platform.

Abbey knelt by Harry's side and looked at the tourniquet and the blood seeping from the leg. Serious but not yet a disaster. She eased off his mask, pushed aside his mouthpiece. Harry's face was pale, his eyes wide, but he was conscious. 'Got you on board now, Harry,' she said. 'Just relax there, take it easy. Everything is going to be OK.'

'Sure thing, Doc,' Harry managed to mumble. Then his eyes closed. Not a good sign. He was hypovolaemic—going into shock because of blood loss.

John suddenly appeared and handed a bag to her.

Technically, she should put on rubber gloves. For now, just for once, she'd wait.

In the bag John had brought she found a pair of

heavy-duty clippers. She slid them inside the tear in Harry's suit and with some difficulty made a cut so that she could see the wound. She winced when she saw it— it was bad.

There was also a pad, which she fitted quickly onto the wound and then tightened bandages round it so that the blood flow nearly stopped. Then she undid the amateur tourniquet. She and John both looked at the dressing for a moment. Yes, it would hold—for the moment.

The next step was to get some plasma expander inside Harry, he must have lost a considerable amount of blood. The sea water sloshing about her knees was now coloured by it. But she couldn't do it here, he needed to be in her surgery.

'The captain says that he'll making straight for port. That right?'

'Yes, it's necessary,' Abbey said. 'And I want an ambulance waiting on the quayside. We'll radio them with more details later.'

'I'll see that it's done.'

John looked up the side of the ship. 'Is that stretcher rigged yet?'

'Coming down to you now.'

This was something John was better at than she was so she stepped back as he organised the stretcher, saw that Harry was securely strapped into it and then hoisted onto the deck. She climbed back on deck herself and hurried along to the surgery. She wanted things to be ready when Harry arrived.

It was hard, taking a dry suit off a semi-conscious

man and not disturbing the dressing on his thigh. Abbey stood back and watched as John and a couple of the divers carefully stripped their friend and then lifted him onto her examination table.

John wrapped him in a blanket and then she took all the readings she needed. Harry had lost a lot of blood. He was suffering from tachycardia, his heart irregular as it tried to pump an insufficient amount of blood. And he was now definitely hypovolaemic, well into shock.

His system was shutting down, she had difficulty finding a vein. But eventually she gained access and slid in a 29-gauge venflon. Then the giving set was erected, and Haemaccel flowed into his system.

She checked the dressing on Harry's thigh. It was leaking—well, it would. But not a lot.

She noticed that the ship was pitching a little more than usual, and the vibration she felt through her feet told her that the captain was making for port with more than the usual speed. Good. She had done all that she could. Harry now needed more expert care. He had lost a lot of blood. On the other hand, he was a young fit man. All she could do now was hope.

'How did we do?' she asked John.

'You did well,' he answered.

'He didn't do his equalisation stops. We'll put him in the chamber, feed him a touch of pure oxygen.'

When they arrived back in Dunlort the ambulance was waiting on the quayside and the launch was waiting by the *Hilda Esme*'s moorings. This was a logistics oper-

ation, not a medical one, Abbey watched as John organised Harry's transfer from ship to launch to ambulance. She saw him give her notes to the paramedic in
the ambulance. Then she felt a great feeling of relief.

'I wasn't sure that we needed a doctor on board,' a voice
said by her side, 'but now I'm completely convinced.'

She turned to see the captain by her side. 'I think
John could have done just as well as me,' she said. 'He
is a very well-trained man.'

Captain Farrow nodded judiciously. 'Perhaps so. In
your career, just how many cases of torn femoral arteries have you dealt with, Doctor?'

She thought. 'I've had quite a long spell in A and E,'
she said. 'I must have dealt with—oh, a dozen cases.'

'Quite. John Cameron has dealt with two torn femoral arteries. I asked him.'

'I've never dealt with one that happened underwater
before,' she said. 'And I don't want to again.'

'That sounds reasonable. Now, when the launch re-
turns, get it to take you to shore. We're not putting out
to sea again today. Apart from anything else, I've got a
report to write, and I hate writing.'

She felt a bit lost when he had gone. John was on
shore somewhere, she didn't know where. When the
launch returned she boarded it with the divers, who
were subdued. The accident had reminded them that
they were all at risk.

She went to her room at the McElvey Centre but
couldn't settle down to doing anything. It would have
been better if there had been work for her, but there was

not. So she read a book for a few minutes, listened to her radio for a few minutes, tried to e-mail her brother and couldn't find anything to say. The accident was still too close.

After half an hour there was a knock on her door. To her amazement, she was presented with a bouquet of flowers by two of the divers. 'From all of us, because of Harry,' one of them laconically explained. 'We just want to make sure that you're around if any of the rest of us has an accident.'

'I was just doing my job!' Abbey exclaimed.

'It was more than a job to Harry. You saved his life.'

Abbey felt a little tearful as they left.

The afternoon wore on. Abbey didn't feel like an evening meal so she went to the dining hall and bought a couple of sandwiches to eat in her room. Then she just sat.

Some time later she had another visitor. It was John and he was angry. He sat on her bed and said, 'That accident shouldn't have happened. They won't own up to it, but I know they were cutting corners again. I've set up a protocol that is supposed to keep them as safe as possible—and they're breaking it.'

'If you're right, they won't be so ready to break rules in future,' Abbey pointed out. 'Now they know what can happen if they're not careful.'

'Perhaps you're right. I'm going to have to talk to them anyway. Abbey, there was no need for that man to get hurt!'

'I know that. Tomorrow you can tell them that. But

that's tomorrow, now it's today. You've come to my room and all you've done so far is shout. I know you hate accidents, so do I. We agree. Now, would you like me to make you a cup of tea?'

She watched as his set face slowly changed. He smiled at her. 'Abbey, you're so good for me. Yes, I'd love a cup of tea. And I'll say one thing before we leave the subject. You were good there. I hope Harry knows it and is grateful. Now, where's this tea?'

When he came in they had been doctor and dive master. But now he had smiled at her and they were Abbey and John and she felt happy to have him in her room.

She made him tea with the kettle that every room had, and then pointed at the window. 'You can tell we're in Scotland, the weather's changed. The sun's out again.'

He walked to the window, looked out. 'So it is. Not a cloud in the sky. Let's go for a walk. I need the feel of dry land under my feet for a while.'

'I know what you mean,' she said. It was odd, the number of feelings they had in common.

'I'll just wash my face,' she said. 'See you down in the hall in ten minutes.' He left, and she slipped into her tiny *en suite* bathroom. After a quick wash, she made an attempt to do something with her hair and a decision that she didn't really need any make-up. Was she ready to go out? Then something struck her. She stared into the mirror but she wasn't looking at herself.

There was a decision to make, and she made it. She left her room, walked down the corridor to where there was a ladies' cloakroom. On the wall there were assorted vending machines. She hesitated a moment, looked round to see if anyone was watching. No, she was alone. She fed two pound coins into the machine, took out a small packet.

For a moment, she stared at its contents. And then she made up her mind. Buying them committed her to nothing. But it left her with an option. If she chose. For that matter, if she was asked. Or John might have bought them himself. She tried to decide how she would feel about that.

Perhaps it was inevitable that they walked along the clifftop to her eyrie. It wasn't something they talked about and decided on. It was just something that happened. As soon as they were out of the town he took her hand, and she was happy to wander along with him. They said very little. For the moment, just being with him made her content.

They met no one on the cliff path. There was no one to watch as they slid down the cliff face to what she had decided was her—or their— own particular private place.

She looked at the little stone seat where they usually sat. It was in shadow. 'I want to sit in the sun,' she said. 'I've got a plastic mac in my bag, we can sit on that.' She took out the mac, spread it on the grass and sat on one end, then motioned him to sit by her.

He sat down and grinned at her. 'This is your eyrie, your little kingdom,' he said. 'Or should it be queen-dom? Whatever it is, you are mistress here.'

'I found it. So it's mine. And we can't be seen from the path here.'

'Good. I like my work, but sometimes, mixing non-stop with people, it gets wearying. I want to be on my own, just for a while.' He paused, and then added, 'And recently, I want to be with you. It's a bit of a new feeling for me, to want to be with someone.'

She wasn't quite sure how to reply to that so she said nothing. Instead, she lay back and stared at the bluest of skies. He said nothing, but a moment later he lay down next to her. They were side by side, close, so close, but only their fingers were touching. After a moment she took his hand, held it lightly. Now things—whatever they might be—were up to him.

He still didn't move for a while. She stared at the sky, saw white seagulls flashing overhead, then she closed her eyes. Beside her, she felt him move, sensed his change of position. Her eyes were still closed but she could detect the sunlight on her lids. Then things darkened. He was leaning over her. She wondered if he would kiss her. But he didn't, not at first.

There was the daintiest of touches, his finger stroking down her cheek from the corner of her eyes to the edge of her lips. Then it slid upwards, stroked the soft skin by her ear, smoothed her forehead and wandered down across her nose.

'That tickles,' she said. 'But it's nice.'

Now he was touching her mouth again, stroking the swell of her lips. She opened her mouth, took his finger and bit it gently. When she released it he didn't touch her face again. Instead, the sky grew even darker, and she knew that his face was approaching hers.

She knew this was a situation she had engineered. She had been more forward than ever in her life before. And John was acting more like a gentleman than perhaps she deserved. Even now she knew she could stop what was likely to happen. For a moment a tiny thread of fear trickled down her spine. Perhaps she should… No. Time to start a new life.

He kissed her. Gently. His lips found hers, for a moment just resting there, completely undemanding. Just their lips touched, their bodies close but still apart. And she felt her entire body relax, she was waiting, wanting, but in no hurry. Soon they would be properly together. But for now he just kissed her.

She lifted one arm, felt for the back of his neck and stroked his hair, letting her thumb rub against his ear. Perhaps it was an unconscious signal to him. But his lips moved from hers, kissed the side of her cheek and then he took the edge of her ear into his mouth.

She couldn't help it. Of all things, her ears had always been super-sensitive and now the thrill of his touch made her entire body shudder with excitement. 'I like that,' she murmured. 'Oh, John!'

He must have felt her excitement. For a moment longer he bit, teased her ear, and then his mouth was on hers. His kiss now was urgent, demanding, and she parted her lips, took him into her in an imitation of an act that was sure to come.

For a moment she felt the weight of his body as he leaned over her, pressed against her. Through the thinness of her trousers she knew, could feel his maleness, his urgency. And she pulled him even closer to her.

Decision time. She took the packet from her pocket, handed it to him. 'I just bought these,' she said. 'Don't ask, don't argue, take them. If you want.'

He groaned, 'But, Abbey I—'

'I said, don't ask, don't argue. Don't even talk.'

For a moment he was perfectly still. And she wondered. But then his hands were at her waist, easing up her shirt, her bra. She heard his gasp of excitement as he saw her nakedness, and then his mouth fastened on her, one breast and then the other, and she felt her body throb with excitement. 'Now, John,' she urged. 'Please, John, now!'

His weight was taken from her, she heard his heavy breathing, the rustle of clothing then the crackle of paper. Her eyes were still shut as she felt him slip off her shoes and socks, undo her belt and slide down her trousers and briefs.

Now she was naked. She could feel the sun-warmed air on her skin, it felt good. It didn't bother her that they were in the open air, not twenty feet from a public footpath, she felt wild, abandoned, she wanted to give her all to this man.

He lay on her, his nakedness against hers, and she wanted him, needed him, body and soul. He entered her and she clung to him, rocked with him, her body the perfect companion to his, knowing what he wanted and needed because it was what she wanted and needed herself.

She felt a sense of desperation in him, almost as if he was confused, looking for something and not being able to believe that he had found it. And in no time at all they came to a frenzied joint climax and he called out her name, 'Abbey, Abbey,' as if asking for something from the gods.

Then they lay there. She cradled his head on her breasts, stroked the long muscles of his back. And after a while she thought about what they had just done.

He hadn't said that he loved her. She would have liked that. Did she love him? Well…getting that way. For the moment, though, she was completely happy.

'That was so lovely,' she said after a while. 'But I have questions. Where are we going?'

'I don't know,' he said. 'But I want to find out.'

She thought about that and then said, 'I'm happy just to see how things go. But there's one thing I want to tell you. You're the only man I've slept with since my husband died. You mean something to me, John.'

That was his chance to say what she meant to him. Even to tell her that he loved her. She was a bit disappointed when he couldn't manage to say anything.

Things could have been difficult next morning when they went off to work on the ship again. They met first, getting onto the launch, when the divers were present. They could be friendly but they had to be formal. Only when they were on ship, setting out to sea, did she see him on her own.

He called in at the surgery, took a quick look round to make sure no one was present, then pulled her to him and kissed her. 'One kiss, just this once,' he said. 'Then we'll be two colleagues working together. We have to be. But, Abbey, I find it so hard to keep my hands off you.'

She laughed. 'Mr Get Things Right,' she said. 'But I agree with you. There's no place for two lovebirds on a diving ship.'

'Only seagulls,' he said, gazing at the noisy white crowd that was following them. 'Abbey, yesterday evening…'

'Yesterday evening was as much my doing as yours,' she said quickly, 'It was what I wanted and I've no regrets.'

'I would hope not,' he said with a wry smile. 'I just want to say that something wonderful happened to me, and I know I'll never forget it.'

Did he know how happy his words made her?

Then his voice altered. 'There's a bit of an alteration to the programme this morning. I'm diving first—I have to inspect where the accident took place, take photographs and prepare a report. Then I've got to make sure that it doesn't happen again.'

'You'll be careful?' she asked anxiously.

'Abbey, underwater, I'm always careful.'

But she still stood and watched as he plunged from the platform, carrying the heavy underwater camera. And she was glad that a buddy was going with him.

It struck her that he was an odd combination—there was both wildness and caution in him. She wondered which character trait was strongest.

He wasn't underwater for long. She watched as he and his buddy rolled over into the diving platform, stripped off their kit before climbing the side of the ship. She gave him a cautious little wave, which he acknowledged with a nod. But he was wearing his mask, so she couldn't see his expression.

He went off to speak to the other divers, and then to shower and dress. She was still standing by the rail when he came and stood next to her.

'Did you find anything interesting?' she asked.

He looked rather unhappy. 'Unfortunately not. It was a genuine accident, it couldn't have been prevented, the men were doing everything properly. I was wrong when I said they were cutting corners, and I've told them that.'

'Accidents do happen. I worked with an A and E consultant once who said that the most dangerous place in the world was home. He broke his arm, climbing out of the bath.'

'Dangerous places, baths. Remind me never to have one.' He leaned his arms on the rail next to hers, and she thought she could feel the tension draining out of him.

'Look,' he said, 'there's the blue sea in front of you, land there in the distance. The sun is shining, you can smell the sea air, feel the wind on your skin. Why do you want to live in London, Abbey?'

'Mostly, because that's where my work is. And it's a great city. Haven't you ever lived in a city?'

'Once or twice, but I've always been glad to move on. I'll be pleased when I move on from here, there'll be something new over the horizon.'

Abbey didn't want to hear that. If he moved on from

Dunlort, would he move on from her? Then she remembered. She had determined for a while to live for the day.

The captain came up to join them, leaning on the rail by their side. 'I've read your report and countersigned it,' he said to John. 'All we can do in the future is pray and hope.'

'The traditional last refuges of the seaman,' John said. 'Often they work.'

Abbey thought this conversation was getting too serious. 'Captain,' she said, 'we were just talking about whether it's better in your life to stay put or to wander. What do you think?'

'Robert Louis Stevenson once said that he would spend his whole life travelling—if he had another life to spend at home. When I retire I'm going to live in Aberdeen. I'll still need to smell the sea.' And the captain was gone.

'I think that sums up the problem,' said John.

The rest of the day's diving passed without any problem. As soon as they got back to the McElvey Centre that evening, Abbey phoned the hospital in Aberdeen. Harry was making good progress, was definitely out of danger, but it would be a while before he could dive again.

Then she made another call about Dave Evans. The news wasn't so good. He had been admitted into hospital with a possibly serious lung infection. 'Thank goodness you didn't let him dive,' the sister said. 'He might have killed himself.'

John was outside, passing the telephone booth. She waved to him and told him the two bits of news. 'Well, I suppose it's all good news,' he said. 'I'm glad Harry's recovering. And I'm very glad that you spotted Dave wasn't fit. But now there are going to be problems. More reports for personal insurance claims.' He shrugged. 'I suppose it's part of my job.'

'Are we seeing each other tonight?' Abbey asked hopefully.

John sighed and shook his head. 'I've got to go to Aberdeen to take the accident report and answer any questions on it. There's a sort of inquiry. I shan't be back till very late and it's the last thing I want or need.' His voice softened. 'And when I think I could be spending the time with you…'

'There'll be other evenings.' She smiled, rather wickedly. 'And you still have memories.'

'Oh, yes, I have memories. Don't you?'

It was her turn to blush.

He handed her a packet of letters, held together by a rubber band. 'There's a pile of mail for you. I picked it up from the office.'

Quickly she riffled through the pile. 'Mostly junk mail. Doctors get no end of it.'

She dropped a letter, which he picked up and handed it to her. In a curious voice he said, 'This one is addressed to Dr A. Linder.'

There was a letter from her nieces, complete with drawings, which she wanted to read. In an abstracted voice she said, 'Linder was my married name, I reverted to my maiden name when my husband died. And my first name used to be Gail—short for Abigail. My husband used it because he said I was like a fresh wind. But I changed that, too. I prefer Abbey.'

'Hey, Doc, did you ring up about Harry?' One of the divers had come to question her.

'I rang. Things are doing pretty well for him, his condition is stabilised, he's well out of danger. But it'll be a while before he can dive again. Will you tell all the others the good news?'

'Certainly will.'

'I must go, Abbey. See you tomorrow.' John muttered a quick goodbye and strode off down the corridor.

Abbey looked after him. He seemed a bit distressed. Probably not looking forward to being quizzed about the accident. Still, he was tough enough to take it. She would have liked to have told him that he could call on her when he got back that night—doctors were accustomed to doing without sleep. And he might need some sympathy if his report did not go down too well. But it was too late now. She would see him on the boat tomorrow.

She went to bed early. She had a feeling that things were working out for her, that there were new horizons, she had a new life and it was marvellous. She was happy and she slept almost at once.

John drove out of Dunlort his face grim, his fingers white on the steering-wheel. He drove for perhaps a quarter of an hour and then, before he reached the main road, he pulled into a lay-by. He got out of the car, walked over the crest of a hill and found himself in a shallow saucer of land. There was nothing but grass and heather, no sheep, so sign of man's works.

The evening was glorious, the sun, the sky, the distant sea. He saw none of it. He needed to be alone with his thoughts.

Only his iron self-control had kept his face straight when Abbey had told him that she used to be called Gail Linder. He knew of a Gail Linder—indeed, had written to her. She had been married to a friend of his, Mick Linder. And he had been diving with Mick when Mick had died.

Whatever the relationship was between Abbey and him, one thing was certain. He had made love to his dead friend's widow.

CHAPTER FIVE

How could they have grown so close without knowing about each other? Well, he knew her as Abbey Fraser, not Gail Linder. She was entitled to change her name. And he, too, had changed his name—she had known him first as John C. Scott. Mick had always referred to him as Scotty. His middle name was Cameron but he had dropped the Scott after Mick's death. The people who mattered knew who he really was, but he hadn't wanted to be known as the man who had been responsible for the death of his buddy. So, both their names were different.

And she had not wanted to talk about her dead husband, and he hadn't wanted to talk too much about his past. There had been no intention to deceive on either side—but they had managed to deceive each other.

In a way their meeting wasn't too much of a coincidence. The world of divers was a small one. Perhaps, as she had kept her connection with the diving world, it had been inevitable that eventually they would meet. But he would have liked to have known!

Now what should he do? He knew that Abbey thought he was responsible for Mick's death. In a way he supposed he was. He still had nightmares about what had happened, wondering if he had done the right thing. Who could tell?

But what to do about Abbey? And he thought of her, of the way they had met, the way that so quickly they had come to like each other, the way they had given themselves to each other so freely. With a shock he realised that, for the first time in his life, he had met a woman who could perhaps persuade him to settle down. A woman for whom he would happily stop roaming. He wasn't certain—not yet. But he was nearly certain.

Did he have to tell her who he was? They were so happy as they were.

It only took a minute's thought for him to realise that he had to tell her. To do otherwise would be to deceive her—and himself.

He wondered how or when he would have to do it, and flinched at the thought.

What would her feelings for him be when she learned who he was? He remembered that she had said that she and Mick had been ready to part, that the love between them had died. But there must be some residual feeling for him. No one could have hated Mick. Be irritated, angry with him, certainly. But Mick had been too much of an amiable idiot for anyone to have hated him.

And Abbey might hate the man she thought was responsible for Mick's death.

And then there were his own feelings. What did he

want? He had been hurt when he had lost his friend. And it hurt him now that he would have to bring misery to Abbey.

No way could he profit from Mick's death. He could not make love to his friend's widow when he had been responsible for his friend's death. What they had together would have to end.

He had made his decision. There was nothing more to think about.

Somehow he managed to drive to Aberdeen and present his report. It took all his strength of mind to concentrate on the report and the inquiry—but he managed.

He got back to the centre deliberately late, wanting to be sure she hadn't waited up for him. There was no light in her bedroom window. He went to bed.

Abbey woke feeling happy, looked at the sunlight in her window and smiled. It was going to be another fine day. People talked about how bad the Scots weather could be, but so far she'd found it fine.

John wasn't present at breakfast and came running down to the launch at the last possible minute. He seemed preoccupied, and when she greeted him his smile was brief. She wondered about the report.

'How was Aberdeen?' she asked. 'Did they give you a rough time?'

'Accidents are always a bad thing,' he said.

When they reached the *Hilda Esme* he said that he wouldn't be seeing much of her that day as he had a lot of paperwork to catch up on. 'Could we go for a walk tonight?' he asked. 'I think we need to talk.'

'Of course. I'm looking forward to it.' She was puzzled. This was a totally different John from the one she thought she knew. He was ill at ease, not confident. He avoided looking at her. And when she looked at him, she just couldn't read what was in his mind. She shrugged. Probably the accident was weighing on his mind.

She had quite a busy day. The captain had asked her if it was possible for her to run a refresher course in first aid for his crew. Her first responsibility was to the divers, but she found some time to do as he had asked. She didn't see John, not to talk to.

When she was having a coffee with the divers, she asked casually where he was. 'He says he's made a mistake, got to put it right,' a diver told her.

'Not like him,' said another diver.

'I'll take him a coffee,' Abbey said.

'Don't. I've seen him like this before. When there's trouble he likes to be left on his own.'

So Abbey didn't take him a coffee. She didn't see him until they took the launch back to the quayside that evening, and then he didn't come to sit by her so as they climbed up onto the quay, she called after him. 'Got a minute, John?'

He stopped and waited for her. He had the oddest expression, seeming both distant and yet imploring. 'You've avoided me all day,' she said. 'If there's anything wrong, I want to know and I want to help.'

'Nothing wrong that can't be put right,' he said.

'Look, Abbey, I've still got things to do. But I need that walk with you. Shall we set off about eight tonight?'

'Eight sounds fine,' she said. She would wait, not think until then. Something was troubling him, she knew. And when she found out what it was, she would help him with it.

She was ready at eight, and almost inevitably they walked through the little town and onto the clifftop walk. Once on the cliffs, where they couldn't be seen, she took his hand. They walked in silence for a while and then she said, 'John, we haven't known each other very long. But I think we're getting to…to like each other.'

She thought of their love-making two days before, and decided that 'like' was too feeble a word. Still, for the moment it would do.

'You've not been yourself today,' she went on. 'You've kept away from me and I want to know why. If there's a problem, perhaps we can sort it out together. We can talk about it. If you…if you're tired of me, well, I can live with it and we can still work together. But I need to know.' Then she kissed him on the cheek.

He stopped, wrapped his arms round her and held her in an embrace so tight that it hurt. But he didn't kiss her. After a while he said, his voice hoarse, 'Abbey, I've never met a woman like you. And I could never tire of you. But…we'll talk when we stop.'

So they paced on together in silence. She still held his hand, but with each step a feeling of dread grew inside her.

They came to their now familiar eyrie. She looked at the patch of grass, remembered how it had been the last time they had been there together. She saw him looking, too, obviously remembering. Then he glanced at her and there was such misery in his eyes that her heart went out to him.

Somehow it was acknowledged between them that they wouldn't sit on the grass. Instead, they sat side by side on the stone seat. Side by side—but not touching.

'We have to talk,' he said. 'It seems like I've known you for ever, even though it's only been a few days. And I know so little about you. You know so little about me. I know we said we'd concentrate on the present and the future—but the past shadows the present. So, please, Abbey, you don't know how important it is to me. Tell me about your husband and what happened to him.'

She thought this was odd, he hadn't wanted to know before. But she took his hand, squeezed it and looked out to sea.

'I got married when I was twenty-four to Mick Linder. He was a bit wild and he made me wild, too. We got married far too quickly. I'd met him at a diving club. He taught me to dive and because of him I did a postgrad course in diving medicine. We were going to tour the world together, him diving and me practising medicine.'

She sighed. 'It didn't work out that way. Most of our two years of marriage he was away. His excuse was that I had to look after my father—which I wanted to do anyway. But instead of staying with me, he got jobs in Australia, Greece, the Caribbean. And we grew apart. He was feckless, had no idea about money.'

'So he was a wanderer, like me?'

Abbey shook her head. 'I don't think so. First, I suspect you'd be good with money. You won't borrow it and then forget to return it. Second, you've got a sense of responsibility—most divers have. Mick didn't.'

'So what pulled you apart?'

'Mick was always chasing after something new and forgetting or ignoring what he ought to have been doing. He was tiring of me. I could see it coming and I knew it was inevitable. I should have known it would happen.'

'It's hard to think of anyone tiring of you,' John said.

She smiled, wanly. 'It happened, though. Anyway, Mick died in a diving accident. It happened on a little Caribbean island. Mick was diving with his buddy, a man called Scotty—it was Scotty's boat. Mick was a bit in awe of Scotty, said he was a hard man. Anyway, they went down together and only one came up. John, you're a diver, you know the rule. You stay with your buddy! But somehow Mick got abandoned. This Scotty wrote to me several times, they were very reasonable letters and he did seem upset. But I blame him! You don't abandon your buddy.'

'That's usually the way,' John said quietly. 'What else?'

'I never went out to the island. The body was never found and the authorities wrote to me to say it probably never would be. There was an inquest, but I didn't go. The verdict was accidental death. Dad was ill, and my brother in Florida sent out a representative to look after my so-called interests.'

'So now it's all behind you?'

She couldn't help it. She started to cry quietly. 'I don't like thinking about it. I know Mick and I were finished—but it seems so sad that he should die. Everyone liked him, and he was harmless really. And sometimes, though not so much recently, I dream about him—it's a nightmare. I see his dead body floating in the sea.'

She felt John flinch.

'He seems to have harmed you,' John muttered. 'This man Scotty—what about him? Do you blame him?'

'I have to. Mick was a good diver so how did he get into difficulties? And you just do not abandon your buddy. So Mick died alone.'

She rubbed the tears from her face. 'Apparently this Scotty was a really tough type. Just before his trip he had finished the Hawaiian Ironman race. Do you know about it?'

'I know about it. Supposed to be the hardest sporting event in the world.'

'Just getting accepted to enter it is something,' Abbey said. 'Those who do finish get a tattoo on their ankle. They're a special sort of man. Mick was always envious of Scotty. Sometimes I wonder if he died trying to keep up with him.'

Abbey took a deep breath, smiled tearfully at John. 'But that's all behind me. Can we talk about something else? You can tell me about you now.'

There was a long silence, and after a while she looked at him, puzzled. 'There's just one thing you need to know about me,' he said.

He lifted his leg, eased up one trouser leg and pulled down his sock. There was a small tattoo. She recognised it, Mick had sent her a drawing of it. The M dot tattoo. She looked at it, her whirling thoughts unable to grasp what she was seeing.

'That is an Ironman tattoo,' he said. 'My full name is John Cameron Scott. You know me as Scotty.'

There was a long silence. She stared at him, her mouth open with horror. Then she said, 'How long have you known I'm Mick's widow?'

'I only found out yesterday. When I saw the letter addressed to you.'

'Right. Will you go now? I want to walk home alone.'

He looked at her for one last moment, then turned and went.

Abbey sat staring at the sea. She had a vision, one she had once had regularly, but which was now mercifully rare. She saw her husband's dead body, still in its diving gear, at the mercy of all the scavengers and predators of the deep sea.

Late that night John was lying on his bed, unable to sleep. There was a scraping noise, he saw a letter was being pushed under his door. He reached for it, decided not to open the door to see who had written to him. He knew it had to be Abbey. He would have liked to have asked her how she was but knew it wasn't a good idea.

Dear John,

We have to work together and we're both profession-als, I'm sure we can manage. But I don't expect to see quite so much of you as before. There's more I want to know and we'll have to talk again. But not yet.

I wish I'd known who you were.

Abbey.

He wished the same thing. If he'd known she was the widow of Mick Linder he could—somehow—have coped with working with her.

Having Mick die when they had been together had hurt. Some people were always ready to believe the worst, they thought he had been responsible. And he had lost a friend, too. He had liked Mick, in spite of all his faults.

Now he realised that running, moving from place to place, was not an answer. Your past would always catch up with you. And now, because of his past, he had lost Abbey.

Only now he had lost her did he realise what she had come to mean to him.

They managed to carry on the next day, working to-gether when they had to. The divers didn't notice any-thing different between them. For them today was going to be difficult.

'There's a set of drums that are trapped, crushed together,' one of the divers explained to her. 'It's going to be hard to free them, we'll have to work from underneath. But it's a job that has to be done. We can't leave them there to rot. They'd poison all the marine life.'

Abbey had noticed before how concerned the divers were about the environment they worked in. 'How much of a risk is it?' she asked.

'John's going down with the first party to organise things. If there are any risks, he'll take them. If things can be made safe, he'll do it.'

Abbey felt a pang, part anxiety, part pride. Whatever she felt about John, she wanted him to be safe.

She watched him prepare to go below with the first set of three divers. When they were about to climb down to the diving platform she went to him and said, 'Is there anything special I should be prepared for?'

He shook his head. 'Nothing out of the ordinary.'

'Good luck, then.' And she turned away.

He returned after a while with the first set of divers, then the second set went down. So far things seemed to be normal—although the crane on the barge wasn't working quite as hard. Getting out these drums was obviously more difficult.

She was working in the surgery when she heard the thump of running feet on the deck outside, heard someone shouting. She frowned. The last set of divers wasn't due to surface for another twenty minutes. And people seemed to be getting excited.

She went to see what was happening. All the divers

were gathered round John, who was talking urgently on the phone line to below.

'What's happened?' Abbey asked the nearest diver.

His answer was terse. 'The drums have moved and one of the girders holding them up has slipped down. Terry Murphy is trapped and his mates can't get him out.'

'How much air has he left?'

'Enough for now, but that's not a problem. We're taking him a couple of spare cylinders, he'll be able to breathe all right.'

'He's been down long enough. If he's down too long, he's in danger of getting nitrogen narcosis. You say he's trapped, but is he injured?'

The diver shrugged. 'We won't know till we get him out,' he said.

Abbey pushed her way through the crowd. John had suited up again and was giving directions to one of the other divers. 'You know I'm an experienced diver,' she said, 'and I'm a doctor. If I can be of any use, I want to go down there. I want no rubbish from you about me being an amateur and a woman.'

Somehow he managed a thin smile. 'If I thought you could help, I'd ask you,' he said. 'But this isn't a medical matter—not yet. It's an engineering problem. I've sent for the oxyacetylene torch. I'm going to have to cut him out. And I'm taking a jack as well.'

'You've dived once already today.'

'I know. But this is an emergency, and I'm still within the safety limits.'

She couldn't help herself, it slipped out. 'You'll be careful?'

'When I'm underwater, I'm always careful,' he said.

He turned to the other divers. 'Four of us are going down,' he said. 'That should be enough. But the rest of you stand by. Mike, you take the telephone, pass on any messages.' He turned to where the captain had just arrived. 'We may have another emergency,' he said.

'Keep me briefed. Let me know what you want and when you want it.'

John and the other three divers slid down the ladder to the platform, where they were handed the underwater cutting apparatus and the two spare air cylinders. They rolled over the side and were gone.

No one moved from the side of the ship. Everyone looked at Mike, the diver who had been given the telephone. Any news would come through him.

Captain Farrow strolled over and stood next to her. 'Waiting is always harder than doing,' he said. 'I did see action a couple of times when I was in the Royal Navy, and after a while you find yourself praying for something, anything, to happen.'

'Do you know what's gone wrong? What needs doing?'

'We have to wait,' said the captain.

Abbey knew that in situations like this it was usual for the point man, the man who was doing the work, who might be in danger, to keep up a running commentary on what he was doing. Then if he was…if he was hurt, the next man would know what to avoid.

Silence for a minute. Then Mike said to the eagerly

listening crowd, 'John's with Terry. He's swapped the cylinders. Terry now has plenty of air.'

More silence. None of the listeners spoke. In their minds they were all below, all with some idea of what things were like down there.

'John says that Terry's trapped by a girder across his thighs," Mike relayed. 'In order to free him John will have to cut through it. To do that he's going to lie on his back underneath the girder. There's hardly enough room so he's taking off his air cylinders and putting them by his side. He hopes the girder won't fall on him.'

There was a murmur of horror from the crowd of divers. 'He's risking his life!' Abbey cried to the captain.

'Possibly he is. You're not surprised, are you?'

There was splashing below them. The relieved two divers hauled themselves onto the platform, stripped off their gear and climbed the ladder to ask how things were going. 'Still waiting for news,' was the terse answer.

There was a message for her. 'Tell the doctor that it hurts but Terry can feel his feet and wriggle his toes.'

A very good sign. It suggested that there was still circulation to Terry's legs. But there could still be internal bleeding into the tissues.

More silence. 'John says he's nearly through the girder. He's positioning the jack to take the weight.'

'Hope it doesn't slip,' a voice said, and Abbey shuddered.

Then there was a shout from Mike, the anxiety in his voice clear to all. 'John! Are you all right? John, what's happening?'

Abbey could feel tension ripple through the crowd.

'So you're OK? You're sure you don't want a couple of—? That's fine.'

Mike looked up and said flatly, 'Bit of a problem with the torch. The girder came down a bit suddenly. It hit the torch and John's burned his shoulder. The suit stopped some of the heat but—'

'He's going to go into shock,' Abbey said.

'He'll get to the surface first,' the captain said calmly. 'He's still got Terry to look after.'

'The four of them are on their way up,' said Mike. Another three divers slipped down the ladder to help their mates over the side of the diving platform.

It was time for Abbey to take charge. 'The two injured ones can climb onto the platform,' she said, 'but the moment they're there I want them on stretchers and hoisted onto the deck. Carry them straight to my surgery, and I don't want an argument from them. Captain, can you organise that?'

'No trouble,' the captain said. 'Do I send for a helicopter to get them to hospital?'

She thought a moment. 'Let me see how they are first,' she said. 'But I would like them on shore quite quickly.'

'We'll head for port the minute they're aboard.'

'Then I'm going to get things ready in the surgery.'

She desperately wanted to be there when John and Terry surfaced, wanted to make sure that John—that both of them were all right. But she knew that her place was in the surgery. She was a doctor and her personal feelings had to be put to one side.

John had given her a quick course on how to work the hyperbaric chamber—she was quite happy about that. She'd examine Terry and have him in at once. Quickly she did the calculations—time underwater, depth of water. Things could have been worse. She hoped that the injuries to his thighs weren't too serious—but she'd have to check before sealing him in the chamber.

Then she wondered just how serious the burn on John's arm was. What would be the effect of seawater on it? For the moment, probably, all that she could do would be to dress the injury and refer him to a specialist burns unit. The bigger danger now would be shock. She strongly suspected that sheer willpower would enable John to get to the surface, to make sure Terry was fine. But once on deck, his over-strained system would collapse. He'd need treatment.

She heard shouting again, realised that the two men had surfaced. Not long now before they arrived at her surgery. She braced herself. She was a doctor. She had two patients to treat, her personal feelings had no part in what she had to do. For a moment she frowned. Why was she concerned about Terry Murphy but terrified about John? After his disclosure yesterday, there was a great void between them.

There was a rattle outside her door and the first stretcher was brought in. Terry Murphy. Most of his kit had been removed but he was still in his dry suit.

Abbey leaned over him and smiled. 'Problems nearly all over now, Terry,' she said, 'I'm going to arrange for you to take it easy for a while. How do your legs feel?'

He knew some first aid—all the divers had been on a course—and knew what she was worried about. 'Just bruised, I guess,' he said. 'There wasn't too much pain and I could wriggle my toes, move my feet. I reckon the circulation was kept up.'

'Good. Any pain in the joints yet? Any stiffness, discomfort?'

'Nothing.'

'You know you're going into the chamber?'

'Anything for a rest,' he said.

'Can you help him out of his suit?' Abbey asked the two men waiting silently by the stretcher. 'Don't let him do too much himself.' She decided that there was little danger from Harry's bruised legs. Then she turned to the second stretcher that had just been brought in.

John. He was also still in his dry suit. As he was brought into the surgery he tried to sit up. Abbey put her hand on his shoulder and eased him back down. 'You just lie there and do as you're told,' she said. 'You're not in charge now, you're in my care.'

'How's Terry?' The words were gasped, he was obviously in pain.

'So far he's good. You got him out in time, you did a good job. Now, have you any other injuries apart from your shoulder?'

'A burned shoulder is quite enough for the moment, thank you.' It was an attempt at a joke.

She looked at his white face, and then had to look away again. She knew he was suffering and just didn't want to admit it. So she had a closer look at the burn on his shoulder and had to stop herself wincing.

The fabric of the dry suit had provided some protection, but through the burned hole in the suit she could see blackened flesh. Very carefully, she touched it with her gloved finger. 'Does that hurt, John?'

'Yes!' She looked up to see him grit his teeth. She hated hurting him. But it was a good sign. If there had been no pain it would have meant that the tissues had been destroyed permanently.

She pointed to a pair of heavy-duty shears and said to one of the divers, 'Can you cut him out of his suit? And try not to move him too much?'

'You're not cutting up my suit!'

'I am,' she told him, 'and you're not objecting.' Then, in a calmer tone she added, 'You know you'd do the same if you were me.' He seemed to accept that.

The first thing to do was deal with his pain. She drew up morphine, injected it and then watched as his face calmed.

The next job was to get Terry into the hyperbaric chamber. He had been brought up too quickly. In the chamber the pressure would be increased to the same as it had been on the seabed then slowly allowed to come up to normal. Any bubbles of nitrogen in his bloodstream would be dissipated.

She watched as the other divers lifted him in. Then

she adjusted the pressure, checked that Terry was OK. No problems there.

Back to John. She knew that there was little she could do for the burn. It needed specialist treatment, possibly skin grafting. All she could do was cover it with a burns gel that she had ready prepared and hope that he'd be able to regain full use of arm and shoulder.

She'd done all she could for the moment. Now all she could do was act as a nurse, keep an eye on her two patients and wait till they arrived at the harbour.

There was a knock on the door, and there was Larry Kent. He looked serious. 'Message from the captain, Doctor,' he said. 'There'll be an ambulance waiting at the dockside, we should be there in about three quarters of an hour. Until then, is there anything he can do, anything you need?'

'We're coping for the moment,' she said. 'You can pass the word—both men seem to be out of immediate danger.'

'I'll do that.'

He half turned, then said quietly, 'We're all very glad that you were on board, Doctor.' And he was gone. A new side to Larry, Abbey thought.

By now John was comatose. The morphine had taken effect and he lay there, his eyes half-closed. At regular intervals Abbey took his temperature and pulse. The effects of shock were slowly receding, but she didn't like to guess what his shoulder felt like.

She had covered him with a silver space blanket as shock could lower body temperature. She had dabbed dry his curly hair, wiped the seawater from his body. When she leaned over him she could see the line of muscle, stretching from neck to shoulder to the upper arm. His skin was sunburned, but soft. She remembered that it was only the day before yesterday that she had stroked that skin, felt it close to hers, smelt its own particular male scent. Then she looked at the dressing she had used to cover his burn. It spoiled things. It smelt of ointments and, underneath, the sickening smell of burned flesh.

He must have felt her presence. His eyes blinked, flickered open to see her leaning over him. 'What a mess,' he said. Then his eyes closed.

She didn't know what he was referring to. The accident? Or them?

Ten minutes late they sailed into harbour. She saw the ambulance on the quayside but there were two paramedics waiting for them in the launch. From the moment they boarded the ship it was obvious that they were accustomed to accidents that had happened at sea and used to transporting people from ship to ambulance. Abbey was happy to leave them to it, making sure that she handed over her notes.

She saw the ambulance drive away, and then took the launch back to the ship. Her work hadn't ended yet. The captain had asked her for a written report. In hospital she sometimes seemed to have spent as much time writing notes as she did treating patients. She had been a bit shocked to discover that there seemed to be just as much paperwork on board a ship.

But finally the report was written and she took it to

the captain. 'You'll let me know how they are as soon as you get any news?' she asked.

'Of course I will.' He looked at Abbey thoughtfully. 'You coped well,' he said. 'It's the second time we've needed you badly.'

'It's my job. I've worked in A and E, I've seen much worse than I saw today.'

'In a hospital you have people to back you up, you have plenty of equipment. Here you had little. I'm glad you were aboard, Doctor. Now…ready to work tomorrow?'

The question surprised her. 'Of course I am. But I thought you needed a—'

'The salvage company that hired us is sending a replacement dive master. He'll only be with us until John is fit again, but the work must go on.'

'Of course,' said Abbey.

She took the launch again and went back to the McElvey. As she walked in the front door, to her amazement she discovered that she was exhausted. And she was ravenous. So she treated herself to the largest meal she could remember having had in Dunlort. Then she went to her room, showered and then lay on the bed.

It had been a full day.

She closed her eyes, reviewed what she had done. Yes, she was quite satisfied with her treatment of the two men.

Then she realised that this wasn't what was bothering her. When she had heard that John was injured, and she had seen the appalling burn on his shoulder, and had had to treat him…how had she felt? He wasn't just an ordinary diver, not one of those she had come to know and like. He was special to her. Why? He was the man who was responsible for the death of her husband. She knew that. In fact, he had admitted it. She should hate him—or at the very least want to have nothing to do with him.

He was also the only man she had made love to since her husband. And she was now coming to realise that it had not been just a simple physical act. It was part of a set of feelings that she didn't care to examine too deeply. It had all been so simple until she had found out who he was!

What was she to do? No, that wasn't it. What was she to feel? She just didn't know.

CHAPTER SIX

NEXT morning Captain Farrow asked Abbey if she'd like to contact the hospital about the condition of John and Terry. He felt that, as a doctor, she'd know what questions to ask and be able to interpret the answers. He'd been in touch over the previous two men who'd gone to hospital—Dave and Harry—and although the hospital had been helpful about John and Terry, he felt he needed to know more. Ultimately he'd require a written report from the hospital for the salvage company and its insurers but for now he just wanted to know how the two men were progressing. Abbey agreed to do this.

She phoned the hospital. Terry Murphy was doing fine, and would soon be discharged. The sister in charge of the burns unit said that John had been lucky, and would not need a skin graft. He'd have a scar and for a while he'd have to try not to strain the shoulder. But all should be well.

'What kind of a patient is he?' Abbey asked.

The sister chuckled. 'Much to my surprise, he's a good one. I can see he's getting restless but he knows that the best thing for him at the moment is to take things easy. He wants to start diving again as quickly as possible. He must be mad!'

'Sometimes I think that all divers are mad.'

'We get quite a few in here. Would you like to talk to him? He's out of bed, I can fetch him easily.'

'No,' Abbey said hastily, 'there's no need to disturb him. Just tell him that the crew has been asking after him and wish him well.'

'So you're not a…particular friend of his?'

'No, I'm not. I'm just his doctor and we work together.'

'Well, you'll know, he was a bit dozy when he came in, what with the painkillers and the shock. We asked him who his next of kin was, and who we could inform about him. He said he had no next of kin. He said if we had to tell someone, then tell the doctor. I presume that's you?'

'I would have thought so,' said Abbey.

'It's a nasty burn,' the sister said. 'We're going to release him in about a week.'

After that Abbey phoned every day to get a progress report. She was always asked if she wanted to speak to John—and she always said no.

Of course, she was still busy. The very next day a temporary dive master arrived to fill in until John's return. His name was Frank Sellars, he was an amiable middle-aged man who showed everyone pictures of his three children. Abbey liked him at once.

'I hear you've been doing great things,' he said to her when they were first introduced. 'The men here swear by you.'

'Just doing my job.'

'Well, if I ever get the chance to work with you, I'll jump at it. Good diving doctors are rare.'

So the work went on for the next two or three days. She enjoyed it and she kept busy. But all the while she was aware that John would soon be back. And she needed to work out how she would deal with him.

The one fact that she couldn't escape was that if anyone had been responsible for Mick's death, it was John. Or she had always believed it was John. But now she couldn't reconcile that idea with the John she thought she knew.

They had three or four cloudy days and then the sun came out and it seemed good just to be alive. The divers sent up a record number of drums—still sticking to the safety rules that John had worked out and Frank continued to enforce. Everyone was cheerful—and Abbey decided to make some decisions. She had come here to start a new life, and after a possibly promising beginning had been thrown back into the concerns of her old life. She didn't like that.

When she came back on shore that evening, she opened her trunk and dug out a thick folder. She eyed it with some suspicion. It had been nearly two years since she had looked at it. Perhaps she should get rid of it. But something stopped her from doing that.

She slid it into a bag, put on her walking boots and set off along the clifftop path. She hadn't been to her eyrie for a while. Not, in fact, since John had told her who he really was, and that he had been with her husband when he had died. Now she had time to spend a couple of hours there.

Her pace slowed as she neared the eyrie, as if she didn't really want to go there. She realised this, and stepped out more quickly than ever. This was something that she had to do.

Once in the eyrie she sat on the stone bench and took the folder from her bag. A moment's hesitation, and then she opened it.

There were three sets of letters inside. Pinned to nearly every letter was a copy of her reply to it. First, a series of letters from her husband sent from the Caribbean. Then a series of letters from the British Consul on the tiny island where Mick had died. Finally, a set of letters from someone who signed himself, J. C. Scott. John Cameron now, she thought. And how her opinion of John Cameron differed from her opinion of J. C. Scott! How could they be the same man?

It was painful but it had to be done. She began to read through the letters, seeing if time had altered her view of things.

It had been a typical madcap Mick scheme from the start. Every diver's half-secret boyhood wish: sunken treasure. Abbey had heard many stories about it.

Most divers' work was very mundane. They surveyed the bottoms of oil rigs, helped reinforce harbour walls, inspected the hulls of ships. But they all dreamed of treasure. Occasionally, of course, their dreams came true. But successful treasure retrieval these days came from large teams in equally large boats with the latest technology to help them. There was no place for two men in a small boat with scuba gear.

But Mick had had an idea. There had been a lot of smuggling between Miami and the Caribbean islands years ago. There were rumours of a smugglers' fast-moving boat coming back from America and caught in a hurricane. It had sunk and the money it had been carrying had never been found, though many people had looked.

Mick had found a computer expert who was fascinated by the story, and who had looked up details of winds and tides and had worked out exactly where the boat had gone down. Well, nearly exactly. But it was a long way from where other people had looked. He hadn't wanted payment—just the promise of a cut if the search was successful. For Mick, this had been proof that the man had been genuine. For Abbey, it was proof that the man was a dreamer.

Mick, of course, couldn't afford to hire a boat, the necessary gear and someone to dive with. But Abbey had been able to. They had been living in a tiny flat, saving their money to put down as a deposit for a house. To be exact, saving her money. Mick had never seemed to have any. He'd had plenty of diving jobs—but, unlike most divers, he hadn't done too well.

He'd argued with her for hours. 'Sweetheart, this is what we've been looking for for years. Find this boat and we can retire. Go where we want do what we want.'

'I don't want to retire. I like my job.'

'We can tour the world! You've got your diving medicine diploma, there'll always be work for you if you want it.'

'I like the world I've got now.'

Mick got up and kicked a chair. 'Like this world? Rotten rainy London? Just look at it!'

Well, it had been raining and, in fact, London didn't look particularly inviting. Mick was between jobs—again. He didn't get as much work as he used to. Abbey deliberately decided not to ask herself why.

'Look, Abbey, let's just have this one last wild fling. And if it doesn't work out, I promise I'll settle down.'

'Give me a week to think about it,' she said, knowing she was being weak.

She didn't get a week. Two days later he drew out all their savings from their joint account. By the time Abbey found out, it was too late to do anything about it.

'Well, I got a chance of this boat,' he said, completely unabashed. 'You were working hard, and your dad was ill. I didn't want to bother you.'

And that was when Abbey realized that their marriage wouldn't last. No one could remain married to Mick. Still, she would try.

Abbey starting reading the letters he had sent her. She had decided she would do her best and write to him, try to support him. She had sent him two or three letters a week. She had got one a week back. If she was lucky.

At first he had been hopeful. He had found a new mate, a man called Scotty. 'You'd like him, Abbey, though he's a bit staid. Does everything by the book. Says he'll work for me for a salary, because he doesn't believe the boat is there. I'll show him!'

There were mentions of Scotty—how tough he was, how he had competed in the Hawaiian Ironman competition. 'Do you think I should try to train for it, Abbey? I'd like to do it.'

Abbey sighed and shook her head when she read that. Hadn't Mick known himself at all? He'd never have been able to train so hard for so long.

Then the letters had got shorter and more infrequent and more bad-tempered. 'Sometimes I can't stand Scotty. He plods, he does everything in the order it was planned. No imagination! Says we have to stand by the sweep plan, says if we don't follow a plan there's no point in having one. He's never had a mad minute in his life!'

Mick's life had been all mad minutes.

Then the money started to run out and he wrote to her to ask for more. 'Can't you get an advance on your salary? I'm sure you could borrow another three or four thousand. I'm even having to borrow from Scotty.' When she refused he was angry, even phoned her in the middle of the night. 'We're married, aren't we? We're supposed to share everything, aren't we? Does that exclude money?'

Abbey turned him down. She knew it was the end of their marriage and she wrote to him to say so.

She never had a reply to that letter. Mick never wrote again.

The next letter came from the British Consul. There

had been an accident. Mick had disappeared on a diving trip. It appeared that he had been diving alone, and
had just not surfaced. No body had been found. He was
very sorry.

She didn't fly out to the island. Her father was seriously ill. And there was no point. The consul had
said that if bodies didn't appear quickly, they'd never
appear—sharks. There would be an inquest and almost certainly a verdict of misadventure. So there
was nothing she could do. And there was the guilt. In
the last letter she had written to Mick, she had asked
for a divorce.

Then there were the three letters from Scotty. As she
reread them she saw that they were dignified, thoughtful. He had told her how sad he was, how much he had
enjoyed diving with Mick. He had told her how lovingly
Mick had talked of her. If she wished, he would come
to visit her in London. He felt guilty. She had written
back, saying that she didn't want to see him, and curtly
asking why Mick had been diving without a buddy.

He had replied to this, 'At times divers disagree as
to what is safe. I thought things weren't safe so I swam
back to the boat. Mick decided to carry on. When he
didn't reappear later, I dived to look for him. But there
was no sign of him.'

She had replied again, saying that it seemed rather a
thin story to her, but she would have to accept it. She
accepted that she was responsible for her husband's
debts. How much did she owe him? Would he, please,
let her have an itemised account?

This time he replied saying that there was no money owing. This was a gamble that both he and Mick had taken.

And that had been the end of the correspondence. Re-reading it, trying to be rational, to be fair, Abbey found quite a few things to wonder about. But the big problem remained. Why had Mick dived without a buddy?

The next day it rained again, and as they headed back to harbour at the end of the day she found herself leaning against the ship's rail, feeling that her new life wasn't as much fun as she had hoped it would be.

Larry came and leaned beside her. 'Missing John?' he asked.

This was too true to be accepted. 'Not really. I think everyone's a bit on edge after the accident.'

He nodded. 'Frank Sellars is a good man, but he's not the man that John was. Abbey, do you fancy a meal tonight? Not a date, just what you once called a couple of colleagues having a drink together. Only dinner, as well as a drink. There's a good restaurant in a town nearby.'

Abbey pondered. She had to admit Larry had been not quite the ladykiller she had suspected when she had first met him. Or perhaps he was, but not with her. Certainly they had got on well together. And why shouldn't she go for a meal with someone if she wished?

'All right,' she said. 'Give me time to get changed and I'll see you in…about an hour?'

'That'll be great.'

'Remember, Larry, two colleagues having a drink?'

'I'll remember,' he promised.

* * *

In fact, she quite enjoyed the evening. They went in Larry's car—a typical Larry car, she thought, a red sports car. After so much time at sea it was a pleasant change to drive over the range of hills behind Dunlort, and along the winding road through the moors.

He took her to a restaurant in a town about twelve miles away and they decided not to have the seafood that it specialised in. They shared a bottle of white wine and chatted inconsequentially about life at sea and what it was like to work as a doctor. Slowly, Abbey relaxed. She had been apprehensive about this, but Larry behaved perfectly.

Then, when the meal was over and they had ordered a coffee, he said, 'So how will things be between you and John when he comes back?'

She hadn't expected that. Sharply, she said, 'Things between me and John will be fine. Why shouldn't they be?'

He shrugged. 'For several days the two of you were obviously very close. Then things seemed to go wrong. I wondered…was it a lovers' quarrel or was it more serious?'

'You seem to take a close interest in my affairs, Larry.'

He was silent for a while then, quietly, he said, 'I'm jealous of John.'

'About me? You can't be jealous! You don't even know me.'

'I think I've got to know you over the past couple of weeks, and I…I rather like you.'

Abbey stared at him, not knowing what to say. This was something that she had not expected. And she couldn't even get angry with Larry. He had been in all ways polite. She sighed. Having a new life was turning out to be more complicated than she had thought.

'Larry, I like you,' she said. 'I think you're a good first mate, as well as a nice man. But whatever there is between John and me, I could never think of you that way. I'm sorry, I truly am.'

She reached over the table and grasped his hand for a moment.

He didn't say anything for a while and then he smiled. 'No matter. I shan't bring this up again, we can go back to being the friends we were before. Now, shall we finish this wine before the coffee comes?'

She said she didn't want any more and he emptied the bottle into his own glass.

After that their conversation went on as happily and as casually as before. They had a liqueur each with their coffee and then decided to go back to Dunlort, even though it was still quite early. 'Are you all right driving?' she asked. 'I think you had more wine than I did.'

'I'm fine. I'll go and pay the bill and I'll see you at the entrance.'

He stumbled as they walked into the main street and she took his arm to steady him.

The sun was setting, was in their eyes as they drove

back to the coast. He remained silent, concentrated on his driving. She thought that perhaps they were moving a little too fast as they roared along the twisting road. But he seemed to be a good driver.

Perhaps it wasn't entirely his fault. Near Dunlort they drove round a particularly tight bend. A farmer must have been crossing and recrossing with his tractor as the road was slippery, covered with mud. And the red sports car skidded on the mud, slid backwards off the road and the rear wheels dropped into a ditch.

The silence seemed deafening. Then Abbey heard birds singing and in the distance the sound of a car engine. She felt her heartbeat slow down to normal. She wriggled in her seat, testing to find out if she was injured. The back of her head hurt just a little where it had slammed against the headrest, but basically she was fine. A bit shocked, but not seriously hurt.

'Are you all right?' Larry asked.

'No injuries at all. You?'

'No injuries either. Sorry about this, Abbey. I suppose I was going too fast.'

Was it her imagination, or did his voice sound a little slurred? Could he have damaged his head more than he realised?

Before she could question him he pulled himself out of his seat, looked up and down the road. When he slumped back beside her his face was haggard, panic-stricken.

'A car comes along this road about every half-hour,' he said. 'And the one that's coming now is a police car.'

'Well, that's good. They can send for help.'

'You don't understand. The local police are having a purge on drunk drivers, they breathalyse everyone who just might have one too many.'

'But you've not had—'

He shook his head. 'I was nervous about tonight, Abbey. I had a couple of double vodkas before I picked you up, and when I went to pay the bill I had another double. They're going to breathalyse me. And I'll fail the test. I'll be banned, and I could lose my job.' Somehow he managed a twisted grin. 'But other than that, I've enjoyed my evening.'

They heard the sound of the car engine, which slowed and then stopped. She thought for a minute and then said, 'Quick, wriggle over to my seat. And keep your head down.'

'What do you mean? I—'

She unfastened her seat belt, pushed open her car door and crouched as she ran to his side of the car. 'Move, Larry! I'll be the driver. I've not had too much to drink.'

He realised what she was planning, and she could see the hope in his eyes. 'You'll do that for me? Abbey, I—'

'Move, Larry!'

When the two policemen arrived they found a slightly distressed couple whose car had just skidded off the road. The woman had been driving, the man her passenger. 'Anyone hurt?' the first policeman said. 'Do we need an ambulance?'

'I think we've got things more or less under control now,' Abbey said.

* * *

An hour later they were sitting in the back of a break-down truck, heading for Dunlort. Larry's damaged car was being towed behind them. 'That policeman knew that I was the one who'd been driving,' Larry said. 'I could tell by the way he was looking at me. And when he told you to be careful, he really meant me.'

'He breathalysed me and I passed,' said Abbey. 'That's the end of the story.'

'Are you going to forgive me for getting drunk?'

'You risked your life, my life, the life of anyone else on the road. Can you forgive yourself?'

'Not easily.'

'Well, I can forgive you if you try to do something about the problem,' Abbey said. 'And I mean that.'

'I'll do what I can.'

The breakdown truck pulled up outside the McElvey Centre. Abbey and Larry got out and the truck towed Larry's car to the garage. They looked at each other.

'I think I'll go straight to my room,' Larry said. 'I've got some thinking to do. Thanks for what you did. Goodnight.'

Abbey walked to the quayside, looked over the harbour at the peaceful *Hilda Esme* at her mooring. It had been an eventful evening, perhaps an early night would be good for her, too.

She turned and went back to the centre. And the first person she saw there was John Cameron.

She looked at him in amazement. 'John! What are you doing here? You're supposed to be in hospital!'

'They don't keep you in for ever,' he said, 'I persuaded them to discharge me.'

'So how are you? How's the shoulder?'

'It's still a bit stiff. I've brought a set of dressings, and I think I can even dive with it.'

She couldn't help herself. 'If I say you can,' she said. 'I'll want to see the hospital report first.'

They were standing together in the entrance hall of the centre, but she felt uncomfortable there. In fact, she felt uncomfortable to be with John at all. She wasn't ready for his return. 'I was thinking of having a coffee in the canteen,' she said. 'Do you want one?'

'Why not?' They walked to the deserted canteen, took a plastic cup of coffee each from the machine and sat together in a corner.

His voice was cool. 'You appear to be having an exciting life,' he said. 'Did Larry's car break down while you were out together?'

'It didn't break down. We ran off the road, went into a ditch.'

'Are you all right? Not hurt?' Now she could hear his concern.

'I'm fine. No injuries.'

'Larry Kent tends to drive too fast. He's dangerous. Had he been drinking?'

'When the police found us I was behind the wheel.'

That appeared to startle John. 'He let you drive his car? He treasures it. You must be getting on with him very well.'

It was obvious from his tone that John didn't like her being out with Larry. Well, she was a free agent, he had no claims on her. And she still hadn't worked out what she felt about John. She was confused. She said, 'If I'm getting on with him very well, that's my business, isn't it?'

Just for a moment she thought she saw a flash of misery in his eyes, but his voice was calm as he said, 'Of course it is.'

She sighed. After a moment she said, 'I don't know why I'm telling you this, because it's really is none of your business. But I've told one lie already this evening and I don't like it. You understand this is in confidence?'

She saw that she had intrigued him. He said, 'I'm good at keeping confidences.'

'Right. So long as you realise that I don't want you to say or do anything. First, I went out with Larry as a friend and a colleague—nothing more. Second, he had slightly too much to drink, we came off the road and I took his place so the police wouldn't breathalyse him.'

'Did he ask you to do that?' John's voice was sharp.

'No. I offered, and I'm glad I did.'

John drank some coffee and then said, 'You're a good friend for someone to have. I hope he appreciates you.'

'I hope so, too. But I won't be driving with him again.'

'Perhaps that's a good thing.' John finished his coffee and stood. 'I'm glad you told me the truth, Abbey. And I will respect your confidence—though I would have liked to have had a word with Larry. Goodnight.'

And he was gone. Abbey sat there with her coffee for a few moments longer, and ran over the conversation she had just had with John. Never before had she had a conversation in which so much had been felt, and yet left unsaid. It struck her that this was because neither of them really knew what they were feeling. Perhaps it would be a good idea if she went to bed.

For the next three or four days, the *Hilda Esme* was to have two dive masters. Frank Sellars was to remain in charge until it was certain that John could dive again. Both men appeared happy with this decision. When they came on board that first morning Abbey told John that when the first set of divers had gone down, she wanted to dress his shoulder and test his movement. He agreed that this would be a good idea.

She was standing by the rail as they cleared the harbour, feeling the ship lift under her as she ran out of the smooth waters. There was the sound of footsteps. Larry came and stood next to her.

'I'd like to invite you to dinner again.' he said, 'in exactly three months' time.'

She looked at him, puzzled. 'Three months' time?'

'And I'll drink only mineral water. I made up my mind last night, Abbey. I'm an alcoholic. I phoned a friend and he put me in touch with AA. I'm going to follow their programme, I'm going to get dry.'

'It'll be hard for you,' she said. 'But if you manage three months without drinking, and if I'm nearby, I'd love to have dinner with you. Good luck, Larry.'

'Thanks, Abbey.' And he was gone.

She thought about him. He was a likeable man and she hoped he had the strength to cope with his weakness. Then, for no reason, she thought of John. There was no comparison. John was strong where Larry was weak.

John sat on a stool in the middle of her surgery, stripped to the waist. Abbey snapped on her latex gloves. She tried to think of John as a patient, as one of the many, handsome or ugly, that she had treated in her time. But it was hard. His skin was tanned but had the clearness of health. There was no fat on him, and when he moved she could see the muscle undulating under his skin. He was an entirely wonderful male creature, and she tried to persuade herself into thinking that that was all he was to her.

He couldn't be the sensitive, thoughtful, passionate lover that she thought he was. He had killed her husband. Hadn't he? Yet once again Abbey's thoughts were in turmoil.

The thick surgical dressing over the burn spoiled the image. She tugged at it gently, making sure that it didn't stick, didn't pull away the new skin forming underneath. And when it did come off, she winced. It had been a terrible injury. When she had first seen it she had been more interested in damage limitation than any kind of treatment, she had known that would be better done in a hospital. Now she could see and think. And wonder what it felt like to have a burn like that, under a hundred feet of water.

'This appears to be cleaning up nicely,' she said. 'There's no sign of infection, the skin is healing itself. Now, see what movement you've got in your arm. Move it up very slowly, lean it backwards. And the moment you feel any pain or tightness, stop and tell me.'

He did as she'd asked. There was far more movement than she had thought likely.

'John, are you sure that doesn't hurt? I don't want any macho pride from you. If it hurts then you should stop. Otherwise you're likely to tear the tender skin and spend twice as long recuperating than is necessary.'

'Honestly, Abbey, it doesn't hurt.'

Perhaps he was telling the truth. She put her hand on the skin just below the burn, felt the warmth of his body, felt a sudden surge of excitement that had nothing to do with medicine. 'It doesn't hurt if I press here?' she asked. And wondered if he knew that her action was just an excuse to touch him.

'It doesn't hurt at all. Abbey, I know about burns. There's no way I would risk permanent damage just so I could dive a few days earlier.'

'OK. I'll renew the dressing and we'll look at it again tomorrow. But so far I'm pleased with your progress.'

'I want to be diving in a week, I need to see how the

men are doing. You can give me a waterproof dressing. And I'll have my dry suit on.'

'You may be able to dive in a week. But that's a decision that I take. And if you do, you act as a supervisor only. You do not do anything but look.'

'I accept that,' he said.

They were both silent for a while as she strapped the prepared dressing securely on top of the burn. There was something strangely intimate about her gentle actions—they both felt it, but neither spoke.

When she had finished he said, 'This is strange. I can't believe that we're doctor and patient, it doesn't feel right. We were getting…close before, and then you found out that I was Scotty—the man you believe responsible for your husband's death.'

'Getting close,' she said. 'That's one way of putting it.'

'After you found out who I was, you put a note under my door. You said we'd have to talk again but not yet. I thought that was right. But I was wondering…do you feel like talking now?'

'Now? Here?' she asked.

'It's a doctor's surgery. It's quiet, it's private. It's an impersonal sort of place, and we need to talk without emotion.'

'Do we? I thought this was all about emotions.'

'Perhaps it is,' he said doggedly. But we need to think clearly.'

Well, yes, they did need to think clearly—some time. But Abbey felt that she didn't want this conversation. It might—it should—lead to some definite conclusions, some idea of her further actions. And she didn't want that, not yet. She wanted to be certain of her own confused feelings.

When she didn't speak, John said, 'Abbey, I've just spent days in hospital. I've had time to think. They gave me painkillers, but sometimes they weren't too effective. But the pain in my shoulder was nothing to the pain I felt thinking about you.'

He spoke quietly, sincerely. She reached out a hand to touch and reassure him. Then she held back. Better if there were no physical contact. Outside medicine, of course. But for a second she desperately wanted to stroke that smooth skin.

'All right, let's talk,' she said. 'But, first, go and put your shirt on and I'll get us a couple of coffees.'

It did no good. He was just as attractive in the white T-shirt. But the warm cup would give her something to distract herself with, or something to hold to her face if she thought her expression was betraying her.

They sat in the surgery, facing each other but not close enough to touch.

'I think I can understand what feelings you might have towards me,' he said. 'I'm the man you feel is responsible for your husband's death. I feel guilty about Mick dying, and more guilty now I've met and got to…like…his widow. You probably hate me, you're entitled to. But even if you didn't hate me, in no way could I let myself benefit by that death.'

Abbey was confused. 'First, I don't hate you. It's just that you've become…different now. There's a side to you that I didn't know. And how could you benefit by his death?'

'Because he's dead, you're free to start another relationship. Whatever feelings there might have been before we knew, now it's obvious there can't be anything between us.' His voice was bleak as he went on, 'You can't fall for your husband's killer.'

'I suppose not,' Abbey said. This conversation wasn't going the way she had expected.

'We've got a week or two left when we have to work together. I think we can do that. And then it's goodbye.'

Goodbye. It was such a final-sounding word. Abbey tried to collect her wildly conflicting thoughts and couldn't quite succeed. A bit of her didn't want to say goodbye to John for ever. Another bit wondered what she was doing, talking so amiably to her husband's killer.

'So we just go our separate ways and pretend this meeting never happened?'

He shrugged. 'You know I don't do long-term relationships. I've never said I loved anyone because I've never felt the need to love anyone.'

'It must make for an easy life.' She couldn't keep the bitterness from her voice.

He recognised her tone. 'Abbey, that time in your eyrie, when we…well, for me it was wonderful. But I'm sorry if I persuaded you to do something that you regret now.'

'You didn't persuade me, it was something I wanted. It was my decision.'

There didn't seem to be anything more to say. They sat and looked at each other for a while, and then he said, 'I'd better go and check how the divers are doing. Are you OK?'

'I'm just fine,' she said.

Abbey sat there when he had gone, running over what had been said, trying to decided what exactly she felt. She was still confused and that made her unhappy. She liked a life of certainties. She had not yet got over the shock of knowing that John had been there when Mick had gone to his death. There *must* be some way in which he was responsible. But what he had just said, and what she thought she knew of him, made her admire him.

Admire him? Surely not the word to use of her husband's killer.

She had tried to start a new life, had wondered if John was going to be part of that life. But then she had found out John's part in Mick's death, and that had to pull them apart. John had realized that. Whatever they might have felt for each other before, it now had to end.

She brooded a little more. And then it came to her that if they were to part, surely it ought to be a joint decision. John thought he knew what she was feeling. Perhaps he was wrong. Wasn't she entitled to a say?

John tried to lose himself in work. Ideally he would have liked to do something heavy and manual: lifting or carrying. But he had sufficient sense to know that it would be counterproductive. His shoulder needed rest. So he ran through the interminable paperwork—checking supplies, filling in orders, countersigning the divers' claims.

The meeting with Abbey had been hard. As ever, he had tried to keep his feelings to himself, but it had been hard. He had told the truth when he had said he had spent many hours in hospital thinking about Abbey. Just remembering her had made it easier to deal with the pain.

Abbey had been something completely new in his life. He'd had girlfriends before, but never one like Abbey. She was the only person who might have persuaded him to stop being a loner. That there could be a future in settling down.

But then he remembered his upbringing, the lessons he had learned. Be friendly, but always keep your distance; never come to rely on anyone but yourself. Too much intimacy meant trouble. It had worked very well for him so far.

Soon this job would be over. He'd move on, probably to some distant part of the world, find another casual girlfriend and forget Abbey.

But he'd always been honest with himself. Forgetting Abbey would be the hardest thing he had ever done.

Abbey was glad that she could work with John. But some of the old togetherness had gone. Sometimes she caught him looking at her, an odd expression on his face, and she wondered what he was thinking. But he never let anything slip.

She remembered how things had been when they had been closer. How she'd loved his thoughtfulness, his sense of humour.

And then she made up her mind. He may have decided that they were to part. But she hadn't. She wasn't giving up on him yet.

CHAPTER SEVEN

'I THINK you can dive now,' Abbey said a week later, as she strapped a dressing on John's shoulder. 'Frank Sellars is going tomorrow. As long as you do nothing at all strenuous, and you can fit a harness to your tanks so that your burn isn't chafed.'

'I can do that. I'll dive at the end of the day, after the last group has come up.'

'And I'm coming with you,' Abbey said. 'I need a dive.'

He looked at her angrily. 'No. You stay on the surface.'

'I am a good diver,' Abbey pointed out. 'I'll be a buddy for you. Don't forget, we've dived together before.'

'I remember. But I'm the dive master, I'm in charge of safety. I decide who goes down and who does not.'

'It won't be like the last dive anyway,' Abbey went on. 'I won't take out my mouthpiece this time, I won't kiss you. So why not take me?'

'You know why not!'

Perhaps she was being cruel, but it had to be said. 'You're worried about being responsible for me after you think you killed my husband. You're feeling guilty. I don't think you need to. John, people can make their own decisions. So I'm diving with you unless you can give me a good reason why not.'

'I'm the dive master. If I say you don't dive, then you don't dive. I don't need to give reasons.'

Abbey was not in a mood to be trifled with. 'If you want to play it that way, fine. I'm the doctor here. I don't think you're fit to dive. I shall enter that opinion in the log and see that the report goes to the captain and the salvage company.'

He looked shocked, he knew the consequences of such a report. 'You'd do that?'

'Well, I might,' she said sweetly. 'But I don't think it'll be necessary, do you?'

There was a moment of flaring tension between them. Then he said, 'I'll send for you when I'm ready to go down.'

He left the surgery, and Abbey let out her breath. That had been close!

She was kept busy, there were the rest of the day's jobs to do. But eventually the time came and he knocked on her door. Gruffly, he said, 'If you have to dive, come and get suited up now.'

He seemed to check her equipment with more than usual care and when she saw the worry on his face she felt guilty. But this was something that he had to learn. She was not just the widow of an old friend. She was a person in her own right.

They splashed over the side of the diving platform

together. And then they were side by side, keeping by the shotline, heading down to the wreck.

Abbey found herself relaxing. The worries she'd had on the surface now seemed far less important. Things would sort themselves out. She even felt there was some kind of communion between them. After a while she bumped into him. He turned so that their face masks were close together and she could his eyes. The eyes were supposed to be the windows of the soul. She wondered what he could see in her eyes. She could see nothing in his.

They circled the wreck, and then he indicated for her to stay outside while he dived into the hold for a moment. She held up five fingers as a sign. He wasn't to be longer than five minutes. He made a ring with his own finger and thumb, the sign of agreement, and then he was gone. Four minutes later he returned, and they set off for the surface together. All had gone well.

'I enjoyed that,' she said as they climbed onto the diving platform. 'How about you? How is the shoulder?'

'The shoulder is fine. And it was good to get below again.' She thought he was calmer than he had been.

'And I wasn't any trouble? We can dive together again?'

'We can if you want to. But I'm still not sure why you want to.'

She thought about that for a moment. 'Neither am I,' she admitted at last. 'Perhaps it's because you forget your problems underwater.'

'But they are still there waiting for you on the surface.'

He was loosening his harness and she helped him ease the strap over where the burn dressing was.

'Do we still have problems, Abbey?' he asked her.

'I think we do have problems. Well, I think I do. I don't know what you think—or feel.'

'Quite often, neither do I. Abbey, you've messed with my head more than anyone I've ever known. But it's not your fault.'

They climbed to the top of the ladder, turned to go their separate ways to change. She said, 'It's nearly three weeks since I found out who you were. That you were with Mick when he died. I'm used to the idea now and I want to talk about it. I want you to tell me every last detail.'

He looked uneasy. 'Abbey, it's in the past. Is that a good idea?'

'I need closure, John. I was trying to forget what had happened and I'd almost succeeded. But meeting you brought it all back and I'm as angry and as unsettled as I was before. John, I need to know!'

There was silence for a moment and then she said, 'And I suspect that you need closure, too.'

'Closure?'

'You need to settle the past so that all there is left are accepted memories—not constant nagging doubts, questions and worries.'

He didn't reply, he seemed quietly agitated. Eventually he said, 'So what do you want with me?'

'I want you to come for a walk to the eyrie with me tonight.'

'That's not a good place for either of us. Two meetings—one pulled us together, the other pulled us apart.'

'But that's where I want to go.'

'Then we'll go straight after dinner.'

So it was decided. She hoped she was doing the right thing.

At eight that night they were walking along the cliff path. So far they had been silent, and he tried to lighten the mood a little. 'What's in the rucksack and do you want me to carry it? Not bringing sandwiches, are you?'

He took a small plastic bottle from his pocket. 'It so happens that I've got a bottle of mineral water that we could drink.'

'I can manage the rucksack. And we don't need the water. It's not sandwiches. It's a file. All the correspondence about Mick's death.'

That shocked him. 'You've still got all the letters?'

'You didn't think I'd destroy them, did you?'

He thought for a while and then said, 'I tend not to keep letters and things. They seem to hold you down and I like to travel light. All I need is memories.'

'Memories can hold you down, too,' she said. After that they were silent again. The hard conversation would start when they arrived at the eyrie.

She still reacted to the beauty of the place, and for a moment they both stood gazing out to sea. It was a wonderful summer evening—but Abbey felt that it wasn't the same as before. She said, 'I wanted to come here to lay ghosts. I loved this place, but now it's haunted by you telling me who you are. I want to get back to what it was.'

His voice was hoarse. 'You know I want to help you, Abbey. But I don't know what I can do.'

She told him about her vision. 'Sometimes, though not often now, I see a picture of Mick, dead, underwater, just floating there. It might have been different if there'd been a body to bury—but everyone agreed that it wasn't very likely that one would appear. That's why I never came to the island. But now perhaps you can help by telling me the truth. The complete, utter truth. I don't care who it hurts, I want the truth. Can you promise me that?'

He took a surprisingly long time to answer her. Then he said, 'If you're sure that's what you want.'

They sat, side by side but not touching. She opened the rucksack, took out the folder and laid it on her lap. 'Letters from Mick to me,' she said, 'and copies of my replies. Letters from you to me and my replies. And the rest is legal stuff, which we'll ignore for now. John, I'm sorry for accusing you of being responsible for Mick's death. But I do need to know!'

His voice sounded more anguished than it had ever been. 'Why can't you just blame me and let things be?'

It was a clue, a hint. 'So there is more!' she said. 'Tell me.'

'Well, you know what I feel. Being underwater is always dangerous. Accidents can happen and—'

'John! What happened?'

He took a breath, stared out to sea. His voice became

flat, mechanical, like a man giving evidence in court. 'You know we were looking for a wreck. The only way to do such a thing properly is to carry out a sweep—mark off the possible area and swim over all of it, metre by metre. It's no good having bright ideas and chasing off where it might be. You have to be methodical.'

'Being methodical wasn't Mick's style.'

'True. He was excited to start with, but then he got bored, and I had to make him stick to the plan. Now, most of the area we were searching wasn't too deep. But at the edge there was a deep trench, dropping perhaps another hundred feet. We knew it was dangerous, not only deeper but there were currents down there. Our wrecked boat—if there ever was such a thing—could have tumbled down the trench. But we'd decided to leave it till last.'

'Seems like the right technique.' Now Abbey was engrossed. In her mind she was there, skimming along just above the sea bottom, perhaps moving off line a little and glancing down into the darkness of this trench.

'That morning Mick was much more irritated than usual. He was worried, upset, said that things were different now, he had nothing to lose. He said we should forget the normal search and dive into the trench. I said we stick to the plan or we give up. We had quite an argument but eventually I won. Well, I thought I did.

'We carried on with the planned search. When we had ten minutes' air left, Mick pointed—he was going to go into the trench. We had an underwater argument—hard when you have to manage with signs. I even got hold of him, but he pushed me off very forcefully. You don't fight underwater. Then he pointed to himself and to the trench, pointed to me and to where I was and then held up five fingers. Clear enough. He would go down into the trench for five minutes, I was to stay where I was. And then he was off.

'I waited five, six, seven minutes, then I went into the trench myself. No sign of him. I searched till I was onto my reserve tank, and then surfaced. Got another tank and went down again. No sign again, but the current down there was vicious. When I was out of air again, I went back to the boat and radioed for help. But I knew it was no good. And it wasn't.'

Abbey felt her heart thudding, was surprised to feel the dampness of tears on her face. John's account had been so real, so believable. She had been there. It was a while before she could speak.

'You didn't tell me any of this before,' she managed to gasp. 'You just said you got parted.'

'I didn't want to seem cowardly, as if I was blaming him. He was dead, he couldn't fight back.'

'But it was his fault, not yours!'

'I should have worked harder at stopping him going into the trench.'

'How? Have a fight underwater? I knew Mick. Once he had a lunatic idea in his mind, nothing could shift it. John, it was his fault, not yours. In fact…you risked your life looking for him, didn't you?'

He didn't answer the question. He said, 'It was the worst moment of my life, climbing into the boat and knowing that I was abandoning him.'

'Will you forgive me for what I thought, and what I wrote?' she asked. 'You did more than you should have, but I blamed you.'

'Nothing to forgive. Just forget it, Abbey. Do you think you've got…closure now?'

'Perhaps. There isn't anything else that I should know, is there?'

'I don't think so.' Perhaps there was just the smallest suggestion of doubt in his voice.

She lifted her head, looked at him directly. She thought she saw a little uncertainty in his eyes. And he was staring at the bunch of letters from Mick.

Suddenly a thought struck her, so appalling that she thought she might be sick. She clutched her throat, moaned with the sheer horror of it. It couldn't be, it wasn't possible, it was sheer stupidity just to contemplate it. But… She stared wild-eyed at John.

'John. Before the dive that day. You said that Mick was worried, upset, and that he said he had nothing to lose. Was he more worried than usual? More upset?'

John avoided her eyes. 'He was always upset when things didn't go right,' he mumbled.

'Did he get a letter from me the morning of the dive? John, tell me the truth!'

The silence between them grew longer and longer. 'Yes,' John said.

Abbey grabbed her file, pulled something from it. 'This is a copy of that last letter I sent Mick. In it I tell him that I want a divorce and that I'll send him no more money. John, did this letter drive Mick into doing something even more stupid than usual? Am I responsible for his death?'

'No!' The answer was roared out. He turned to her, seized her shoulders and shook her. 'Abbey, that is madness! Whatever happened was Mick's own fault. He was an experienced diver and he was his own man. He made decisions so he had to take the consequences. You're out of the picture entirely!'

But the vision came back, stronger, more distinct than ever. There he was, floating underwater, already dead. He rolled, propelled by the current, and an arm stretched out and waved. And she had driven him to it!

She cried for the mistake she had made. She cried for the memories of Mick, a man with grave faults but also capable of love. She cried because she had misjudged John.

He held her, not too tightly, and after a while started to stroke her hair. It was so comforting lying here against him, his arms round her, feeling his warmth, the muscled hardness of his chest and back. And slowly her life slid back into order and she was becoming herself again.

She leaned back, he released her at once. Then he took a handkerchief and the bottle of water from his pocket. He poured a little water onto the handkerchief, used it to wipe her face. It was cool and refreshing and it made her feel better.

'Thank you,' she muttered. 'May I have a drink of water?'

He offered her the bottle, and she took a drink from it.

Then he put an arm round her shoulders and she leaned against him again.

'Things seem clearer now,' she said. 'I know what happened, I know what part I played in it, and I feel sadness but no guilt. I feel a bit bad about you, but I know you'll forgive me. And so it's all at an end. I've got my life to live now.'

She opened the rucksack and held it between her knees. Then she took the file of letters on her lap and started to tear them up, one by one. Scraps of paper dropped into the opened rucksack.

'What are you doing?' he asked.

'I'm tearing up these letters and tearing up the past and my grief. I won't have visions of Mick any more. That part of my life is over. I'll burn these bits when I get back tonight.' She thought for a minute and then said, 'How do you feel?'

'Better. If you say that you feel better. There's something of a weight been lifted from my shoulders.'

'Good.' Abbey didn't know why but she felt renewed, clear-headed, as if the future was in her grasp. Her new life was starting—again.

'Last time we met here, you told me who you were,' she said, 'and that started us down a bad road. But the time before we lay naked on the grass there and you brought me pleasure I'd never felt before. We're back to that stage now, John. There's just you and me. Do you think things might be different? There's no hurry. I just want to see how things go.'

He shook his head as if distressed. 'I just don't know

what I feel, Abbey,' he said. 'All my life I've been a loner, self-contained. Then I met you and for a while I wondered if things might be different. If I could share everything with just one person. But then things changed. Mick came up—I'm not blaming you or me. But finding out about him and how we were connected has taught me that life is never that simple. There's always a catch. I'm better off not making commitments that might turn out differently to what I expected.' After a moment he added, 'And I never could…profit by the death of a friend.'

She leaned over, pulled up the leg of his trousers and looked at the Ironman tattoo there.

'Always the Ironman,' she said, bitterly. 'Always in control, letting nothing affect him. John, do you know that I was beginning to love you?'

She looked at him directly, and he had to look away. 'You love me?' He thought about that. 'Abbey, I don't think I've ever told anyone I loved them.'

'Try it,' was the dry response. 'It's good for you.'

This was obviously somewhere he didn't want to go. 'You'll get over me, Abbey. And I'll always be glad I've met you. You'll be one of the memories that I…' He looked at the now darkening horizon. 'Shall we get back? It's getting late and we've had a—'

'Hard evening,' she said flatly. 'You go back. I want to stay here just five minutes more.'

He looked at her, irresolute. 'Are you OK?'

'I'm fine. Better than I've been in months.'

He stared at her a while longer and she added, 'Honestly, John, I'm fine. You can fall in love more than once. I'm sure I will again.'

And then he went. Abbey stared down at the pile of torn paper.

John walked back quickly, not noticing the beauty of his surroundings. He had a lot to think about and for a man who normally had no doubts it was disturbing.

He was surprised to find that, in one way, he felt better. He had meant to keep the exact circumstances of Mick's death a secret. But having told Abbey, he felt somehow relieved. It was a story that he had needed to share.

And he thought that perhaps Abbey felt relieved, too. She had been married to Mick, she knew what he had been like, and she must have suspected that there was more to the story. Well, now she knew. He hoped she had found the closure that she needed. He thought that perhaps she had. But he wished that someone else could have told her.

Then he thought about love. People were always talking about love, reading about it, singing about it. Not him. He'd never felt the need.

He tried it to himself, spoke out loud. 'I love you… I love you…' Easy enough to say, though the words seemed a bit strange when he said them aloud.

He thought of the way Abbey had looked at him when she'd said that she was beginning to love him. Had she expected a reply from him? Had she expected him to say that he was beginning to love her, too? After all, they had made love.

Did he love Abbey? Did he need or want the trouble, pain, worry that that kind of commitment might bring? True, it might bring happiness but wasn't he happy now?

He tried speaking the words again. 'I love you.' They sounded hollow.

This was silly. The divers would be having their rationed drink about now. He thought he'd go and join them.

Things were easier for Abbey on the boat next day. John greeted her with a grin, asked if she had got rid of her papers. All right, if that was the way he wanted to play it. As if nothing had happened. Perhaps it was the easiest for them both.

'I polluted the atmosphere,' she said. 'I stuffed them into the stove.' Then she added, 'And it made me feel much better. There was a sense of something ending.'

His smile then was a bit forced. Well, let him suffer.

After yesterday's wonderful weather, today was a bit of a change. There was a cool wind blowing, the occasional sprinkle of rain. When they sailed out of the harbour, the *Hilda Esme* started to pitch and roll.

Abbey had just gone into the surgery when she heard Captain Farrow come up to speak to John. 'Are you happy diving in this weather, John?'

She could hear the amusement in John's voice. 'In weather like this I'd rather be underwater than on the surface. No waves down there. But I'm a bit worried about getting in and out of the water. That can be difficult. Even dangerous.'

'That's what I thought. Well, the forecast is that

there's going to be a storm. I suspect we'll be giving up early, heading back for harbour. Sorry that the divers can't try for their bonus, but that's my decision.'

'I agree. Even if you were willing to hang on, I'd stop them diving if it got much worse than this. But we might get in a few hours' work first.'

After that Abbey saw the weather deteriorate. The wind grew even stronger. John was on the telephone and ordered a set of divers to come up before they had finished their allotted time. Once they were on board he arranged for the inflatable diving platform to be pulled on board and secured against the coming storm.

The first chill rain hissed across the deck and the distant line of land was lost in a murk of grey mist. The *Hilda Esme* started to roll and pound on the heavy seas. The captain ordered the moorings cast off, got under way and turned the ship's bow into the wind. This was going to be a real storm.

Once she had seen that the divers were safe on board, Abbey went back to her surgery. As a matter of course she had always made sure that there was nothing loose, either on any of the surfaces or in any of the drawers. But she checked everything again. This was the worst weather she had experienced yet. It seemed as if the deck was heaving and as she moved from side to side in the surgery she had to steady herself by hanging onto the nearest handle.

Her phone rang. It was Larry. 'Captain's orders, Abbey. Will you not go on deck without letting us know first, please? We'll get you an escort.'

'OK, Larry, that's fine. But if I'm needed for any-thing, I expect to be told. Incidentally, I've never suf-fered from seasickness.'

'Aren't you the lucky one? We'll let you know if there are any medical problems.' He hung up.

She moved to one of the portholes and looked out. She winced. The sea was rough! Well, that wasn't her problem. All she had to do was sit tight and wait the storm out.

Adjoining the surgery was a tiny cabin—just a bunk and a washbasin. She could sleep there, be quite com-fortable. She lay on the bunk and stared at the ceiling. She had brought nothing to read and there was no radio in the surgery. What she could do was think. Last night had been nearly too much for her. Never before in her life had she been hysterical—and she'd had more than a few personal traumas. But last night had been different.

She had wanted to be alone. But it was only five minutes after John had left before she'd walked back. She hadn't spent any time thinking, she would keep that for later. Deliberately, she had walked so fast that she had been panting and out of breath when she'd got back to the McElvey Centre. She had showered, made herself a drink, then sat and considered just one thing.

How far was she responsible for the death of her husband?

She thought of the man she'd thought she'd loved and had married. It had been a whirlwind courtship. Well, that had been Mick's style. He'd believed life was there to be grabbed, no need to plan anything, never mind the consequences, everything would sort itself out. So after six breathtaking weeks she had married him.

Had she been in love? He had been witty, handsome, a breathtakingly exciting man to be out with. Women had stared at him, their feelings obvious. For a while Abbey had basked in this, he had been *her* man. But then she'd tired of it. And she'd tired of it even more when it had become obvious that Mick had needed and encouraged this regard.

Mick hadn't been able to settle down. For him a quiet night at home, doing nothing much but being with his wife, each enjoying the other's company—that would have been an evening wasted. And he hadn't been able to cope when things had gone wrong. They had tried to buy a flat but the sale had fallen through. Abbey knew that these things happened, but Mick had been enraged for a week.

Now Abbey had to face up to it. Their marriage had already been doomed when he'd taken their money and gone off searching for treasure. She knew he'd loved her in his way. But she had only been a small part of his life.

Had it been fair of her to write that letter to him? She had torn it up now, but she could remember what it had said. She lay there thinking, knowing that this was the crux of the matter. She knew her breathing was faster, could feel the slight beading of sweat on her forehead. And slowly the realisation came. She was guiltless. She had tried to make the marriage work, she had suffered, eventually she'd had enough. She had written saying she had no more money—which was true—and that she wanted a divorce.

Even at that late stage she'd known that had he come back to England, promised to try to make things work out, she would have taken him back. But he hadn't. Typically, Mick had done something foolish. And perhaps for the first time in his life he had paid the full price.

Abbey realised she was guilt-free. And she knew that never again would that vision of the drowned man haunt her dreams. Now she had closure with Mick.

The trouble was, there was still John. She realised that her relationship—or lack of it—with John was much more important than Mick. But she just couldn't start thinking again. So—another first for her—she reached for her doctor's bag and took a sleeping tablet. Two minutes later she fell asleep.

The noise of the storm suddenly got worse. Someone had opened her door and come into the surgery. 'Abbey!' She recognised the voice and slid off her bunk. It was John. She should have known better, but her heart started racing. Why did he still have this effect on her, after all they had been through? After all he had said?

He was wearing oilskins, they were wet through. He had another set of oilskins in his arms and held them out to her.

'How are you coping with this weather, Abbey? It's rough, you might feel sick and I—'

'John, I've never been seasick and I've been in worse storms than this! So don't worry about me. Right?'

'Right,' he said. 'Sorry. Now, we're not going to make for the harbour. The captain's had a report that conditions there are dangerous. So we're going to ride out the storm at sea. He's much happier about that.'

'What about the divers?'

John nodded. 'They're happy. They'll get extra money for having to stay on board. There's a bunkroom where we can sleep and there's no shortage of food. Which is one reason why I came. Like to join us for dinner?'

With a start, she realised she was hungry. 'I think I would,' she said. 'but I'm not supposed to leave the surgery unless I'm escorted.'

'I'm delegated to escort you. Put these oilskins on and let's go.'

'Just a minute.' She took a packet of pills from a cupboard. 'Are any of the divers feeling queasy?'

He frowned. 'I hadn't thought of that. I suppose it's possible. A couple of them seem a bit quiet.'

'I'll bring some stuff, have a quick word.' She took the oilskins. 'All right, let's go.' He opened the door for her.

She hadn't realised just how violent the seas had become. The deck heaved even more. Visibility was down to a few metres, the waves were foam-flecked and the wind howled through the superstructure. Although she had a firm grip on the rail, she was glad of John's strong arm round her waist, holding her up. She made slow progress down to the divers' mess hall, and when they got there her oilskins were drenched.

The divers were philosophical about the storm, these things happened. Abbey asked if any of them were feeling at all queasy. A couple admitted that they had felt better so she gave them Dramamine.

She shared a meal with them and then John took her back to the surgery. 'Are you going to be all right here on your own?' he asked. 'If you want, I could stay here and—'

'John, I'll be fine. In fact, a few hours on my own might be a good thing.'

'Right then,' he said, looking as if he wanted to say more. 'Well, if you need me, or anything, I'll be with the divers. Don't come. Phone me and—'

'I know where you are and I can't see any reason why I should need you. But if I do, I'll phone.'

He looked at her a moment more, then went. Abbey took off the soaked oilskins and hung them to drip. For a minute or two she wandered around the surgery, but there was absolutely nothing left for her to tidy. She wondered about phoning Larry, asking him if he had a book she could borrow. Then she thought better of it. Larry was first mate of the *Hilda Esme*. He had worries enough at the moment. She could phone John. No, she didn't want to do that. So she lay on her bunk and thought about him.

She didn't love him. She almost loved him, she could easily get to love him, but she didn't fully love him. Not yet. Well, that was something to be thankful for. And he had said that he couldn't—wouldn't—love her. Certainly, he couldn't say it. It didn't seem too hard to Abbey. 'I love you... I love you...' she muttered to herself. There, it was easy. If you meant it.

But John didn't mean it, wouldn't say it. He had told her they weren't to be together. She'd be one of his memories. That was small comfort.

One thing she did know about him. Once he'd made up his mind, he wouldn't change it. So John Cameron wasn't for her. She had to give up all thought of that, no matter how much it hurt.

Too much emotion was tiring. She rolled over on her bunk and fell asleep.

CHAPTER EIGHT

'DOCTOR FRASER!' A different male voice, this time the Captain's. Abbey frowned, what could persuade the Captain to come here when he could call her to the bridge?

'Coming,' she called. She yawned and stretched, and then opened the door.

Two people were in the surgery, Captain Farrow and John. Both were in streaming oilskins, both with serious expressions on their faces. 'Is there a problem?' Abbey asked.

The captain spoke. 'There is. I don't know if you can help us but I want to talk about it. You know there's an oil rig about twelve miles away?'

'I've seen it,' Abbey said. 'Why?'

'We've just received a radio message from them. They've had a bad accident on board, three men injured. The weather is far too rough for a helicopter to land on their pad and will be too rough for some hours. You are the nearest doctor and they need one badly.'

'What about the paramedic there?' John asked.

'They're very well trained. I've worked with them, there isn't much they can't handle.'

'Ah, the paramedic,' the Captain said. 'You mean the one with the compound leg fracture? He's one of the injured three. All they've got available is men with first-aid certificates. And that's not enough.'

'Look,' John said angrily, 'I know what you're thinking about and it's just not possible. No way can Dr Fraser be asked to go aboard the oil rig. It'll be dangerous, it might even be impossible. I'll go in her place. I can do everything she can.'

'Not everything,' Abbey said icily. 'Your skills are excellent, but they're limited.'

He looked at her as if he had difficulty believing what he was hearing. 'I'm a navy paramedic and I—'

'And I'm a trained A and E doctor. I decide whether I want to go or not.'

'Just a minute!' The captain's voice was sharp. 'The first thing to remember is that it's I who decides who is to go. Or if anyone goes. I'm the captain. I make decisions. Is that clear?'

'Yes, Captain.' Abbey and John spoke together.

'I'll radio the oil rig and tell them that we're making for them. When I see what conditions are like I'll decide whether it is possible to put anyone aboard. If I decide it is possible, Dr Fraser can decide if she wants to try what will be a very dangerous operation. There will be no pressure put on her—in fact, I will advise her that it's not a good idea.'

'If she goes then I'm going to…' John started

It could have been quite funny. Abbey watched the faces of the two men, saw that the captain was getting even more angry, and that John had the sense to realise that. He moderated his tone and said, 'I think it would be a good idea if I went, too, Captain.'

'I'll think about that. It will, of course, leave me without any medical cover. But still…'

'While we're making for the rig, do you think I could talk to whoever is in charge?' Abbey asked. 'I need to know what the situation is. Possibly what medical kit to take.'

'You won't need to take any medical kit,' John said. 'That is, if you go. The oil rig medical centres have everything, they're based on the medical centres in warships. They're better equipped than many hospitals.'

'Except for doctors,' Abbey said.

'Dr Fraser, I'll leave you to think about things,' the captain said. 'I'll set a course for the oil rig, we should arrive there in about an hour. Only then will I decide if it's possible to put you aboard. I say possible, but even if it's possible it will be dangerous. Let me emphasise again, you are under no pressure to attempt this. In fact, I—'

'You son will be a doctor soon, Captain. In these circumstances, would you expect him to go aboard? And, please, don't say things are different because I'm a woman.'

He scowled at her for a moment. Then he said, 'Yes, I would expect him to go aboard. Dr Fraser, I'll have the radio operator patch you through to the oil rig. I'll come to see you when we are nearer.'

He turned to go, said, 'Mr Cameron, come with me, please.' And the two of them left.

An exciting life, Abbey thought. She went into the little cabin, brought out what she called her emergency pack. It was tightly wrapped in a waterproof bag, had a strap that would hold it tight to her back. She suspected she was going to need it.

Five minutes later her phone rang. 'Patching you through to the oil rig now, Doctor,' a voice said. 'You're speaking to a Mr Gary Flynn, the duty officer.'

'Hello? I'm Dr Abbey Fraser.'

There was silence for a moment and then a surprised voice said, 'You're a woman.'

'I know,' Abbey said. 'Now we've settled that, can you tell me who is injured and how badly?'

'Yes, right, well, of course. Three people hurt. We've got them in bunks in our sick bay but we just don't know what to do next.'

'Tell me what you can see of their injuries,' Abbey said.

Gary did so. And at the end of the conversation, Abbey knew she was going to have to get aboard the oil rig. She gave a couple of general instructions and then said, 'Keep them warm and comfortable. I'm coming and I'll do what I can when I get there.'

'We need you,' Gary said.

Her next visitor was Larry, about half an hour later. 'Captain's compliments, Dr Fraser. Would you join him on the bridge? I'm to escort you there.'

She noticed that in this time of crisis everyone had

suddenly become very formal. She suspected it was the captain's navy training. And she rather liked it. It made her feel she was part of an efficient, cohesive unit.

The storm had got worse. The *Hilda Esme* was bucketing through the seas, throwing a bitter cold spray over the decks. It shouldn't have been dark yet, but there was little light in the sky. Until she looked over to port and saw the oil rig. Lights shone from everywhere, it was like a Christmas tree. And it was vast! She had never quite appreciated just how large an oil rig was.

She had to hang onto the handrail as she climbed up the stairs to the bridge. And once the door had been slammed behind her, she found herself again in the company of the captain and John.

'Before you say anything, Captain,' she said, 'there's a young man aboard the oil rig who could die. If you permit it, I want to try to go aboard.'

'Now, why isn't that a surprise?'

She saw John scowling at her, but he said nothing.

'I've been in touch with the people there,' Captain Farrow said. 'We're going to move round to the lee of the rig, where there might be a bit of shelter. I'm going to have to sail very close to those great girders. I'd hate to hit one but I think we can manage. Mr Cameron here suggests that we lower the diving platform and you both wait there. The rig will lower what they call a cage. You'll just have to jump aboard.'

'Sounds fun,' said Abbey, though she was quaking at the thought. 'Did you say Mr Cameron was coming, too?'

'I think you'll be safer with him. Now, you understand that at times this cage will be half underwater, and at others it'll be feet above your head. The winchmen are pretty skilful, but no one can predict what these seas are going to do. You'll just have to judge your moment and jump. There'll be a couple of strong men to haul you to safety. But…there's that risk.'

'Let's go,' she said.

She stayed on the bridge and watched as the Captain skilfully manoeuvred his ship round to the lee of the oil rig. Perhaps things were a little quieter here, the storm not so violent. The captain had earphones on now, was in constant contact with the winchmen. John left the bridge, came back five minutes later to say, 'The diving platform's rigged. But it's bouncing about.'

'Then let's get started. Dr Fraser, you know you're going to get wet through? And if there's an accident those oilskins will only be in your way?'

She indicated her emergency pack. 'This straps to my back. It's a complete change of clothes and a toothbrush.'

'Good. You'll be fitted with a lifeline and a lifejacket. I hope you don't need either. Good luck.'

And that was that. Suddenly Abbey realised the danger she might be in. It didn't seem quite real.

Carefully she made her way down from the bridge and with John's helping hand walked along the deck to where the landing platform had been secured. She glanced upwards. The rig seemed to stretch for miles above her. Even the platform seemed way out of reach.

Suddenly everything was brighter than the brightest day. Someone on the rig shone two powerful beams on the bobbing platform, the side of her ship, the giant girders. It made everything surrounding seem pitch black and focussed everyone's attention on the little strip of sea.

Someone took off her oilskins and she was wet through almost instantly. A harness was fastened round her waist, a safety line attached to it. 'You know how to release this when you're safe?'

'I know.'

Then the lifejacket. 'You know how this inflates automatically when you pull this lever?'

'I know.'

'Let's get down onto the diving platform,' John said. 'I'll go first.'

One last glance around. It seemed that all the divers and many of the crew had come out to watch. 'Don't get wet, Doc,' a voice shouted, and she managed a smile and a wave. She didn't feel like smiling or waving. She was wet, cold and terrified.

Down the ladder onto the diving platform. The ship heeled and she needed all the strength in her arms to hang on. A wave hit the ship, the ladder jerked and Abbey fell four feet onto her back, splashing in the water sloshing around and over the platform.

John knelt by her, put an arm under her head. 'Abbey, are you all right?'

'I'm winded and angry,' she said. 'But, yes, I'm all right.'

'You shouldn't be here!'

She rolled over, struggled to her knees. 'Neither

should you. You've still got a badly injured shoulder, this is going to do it no good at all. Why are you so worried about me?'

'Because I've been involved with one…accident with your family already. I don't want to make it two.'

'Now you're being ridiculous. John, I'm my own woman and I make my own decisions. Now, help me up. Just with your good arm!'

Even in that desperate situation she thought that she would have preferred it if John had thought of her, not her family.

He took her arm, hauled her upright. 'They're dropping the cage now. You jump first, I'll be behind you if anything goes wrong. If it isn't the right time, don't jump. It'll come down again.'

She looked up. The cage was just that—a structure of steel tubes, double doors now open. Inside, two men in dark outfits knelt by the doors.

The cage whirred down quickly, then stopped just above them. The winchman above was trying to position it exactly—but it was hard with the ship heaving as it was.

Then he got it nearly right. The cage splashed into the water, a foot from the platform. The two men were up to their thighs in the sea. But the wave was passing, the platform dropping slowly. 'Jump!' shouted John, and thrust her forward.

And, in fact, it wasn't too hard. But she landed sprawling on the cage bottom, was instantly hauled to her feet by the two men. She was hustled to the back of the cage, strapped to some kind of harness and told not to move.

Now it was John's turn. He stood there, waited till the right moment then casually stepped across into the cage. Hmm! Abbey thought, irritated.

Her lifeline was unfastened, as was John's, and both thrown back out of the cage. Then there was a whirring sound and they were pulled upwards with what seemed amazing speed. The *Hilda Esme* was there below her, she could see the divers looking up at her. Then they were swung aboard and the cage clanged down.

Strange. The deck wasn't heaving. But the wind was still blowing, the rain still cascading downwards.

'You both did well there,' said one of the men out of the cage. 'Not as hairy as I had expected.'

'It was hairy enough for me,' said Abbey.

A man came rushing out of a nearby doorway, held out his hand. 'Dr Fraser. Good to have you aboard. I'm Gary Flynn, the duty officer. We spoke earlier.'

'This is John Cameron,' Abbey said. 'He's here to assist me.'

'Right. Well, come inside, we'll get you dried off. Would you like something to eat or drink?'

'I'd like to get into something dry and almost sterile, and then see my patients,' said Abbey.

'No trouble. I'll be staying staying outside the sickbay door. Whatever you want—and I mean whatever—you ask me and if we've got it you can have it. Dr Fraser, we're so glad to have you aboard.'

'Let's hope I can be of some use,' said Abbey. 'Now, for a start, what happened?'

'Three men. Two were working on a gangway, one just walking along it. The one just walking was our paramedic. For some reason the gangway gave way— we don't know why yet, but there'll be an enquiry. The three men fell and smashed into the ironwork below. Two are conscious—just. The other has an injury to his head. We've dressed it as best we can but he keeps drifting in and out of consciousness.'

'I don't like the sound of that,' said Abbey.

They had been walking along a corridor and after the chill outside Abbey found it pleasantly warm. The turned into a little suite and Gary said, 'This is our sick bay. It's very well equipped in case of emergencies, but we usually like to send out injured off by helicopter.' Hastily he added, 'Not that we have many injured.'

Gary looked at the two of them uncertainly. 'I'm afraid there's only one lockerroom,' he said. 'I've put in a pile of—what are they called, look like pyjamas—scrubs, that's it. All sterile. There's two of you and we—'

'I'll shower and get changed first,' Abbey said. 'Then Mr Cameron can do the same.' She smiled sweetly at John.

There was a shower, more powerful than Abbey had ever felt. She washed herself, used a couple of the great pile of towels then dressed in green scrubs, with her own dry underwear from her emergency pack. Then she went out, nodded at John and Gary.

'See you when you're ready,' she said to John. 'Now, where are these patients?'

She was very impressed by the sick bay. The one on the *Hilda Esme* was well fitted out but this was medical luxury. Still, equipment was no good without a doctor. There were just four beds, three of them in use. Everyone seemed to be comatose.

Triage. Prioritise. 'Did you take notes of what treatment you've given these men?' she asked Gary, 'and what time you gave it?'

Gary shrugged. 'Not really. But I can remember exactly what we've done. Eric there had lots of bruises, cuts, things that didn't seem too complicated. We've cleaned up the cuts, put sticky plasters on them. But the worst was that he complained of bad pain in his arm and shoulder. It might be broken or something. I gave him an injection of pethidine into his arm.' Gary swallowed. 'I've never given an injection before. I didn't like it.'

'How much did you give?' Abbey's voice was anxious.

'I gave what Peter Nellist told me to. He was in agony, but he stayed awake long enough to give a couple of instructions. He wanted morphine himself, he told me how to give him it and I did and he went unconscious.'

'You did a good job, Gary. This is the paramedic?'

Gary winced. 'That's Peter Nellist, our paramedic. Look at the blood round his leg. He was in agony, you could see the white of the bone in his leg.'

Sharply Abbey asked, 'Did you put on a tourniquet, or anything like that to stop the bleeding?'

'No. Just dressings, which we tried to keep tight. I think we hurt him.'

'Hmm. And last?'

'Perry. Hit his head on a post as he fell. There's that large gash in his head, which we dressed, but I think he might have fractured his skull. We just don't know. Do you think it's affected his brain?'

'I don't know.'

A voice behind her said, 'What can I do to help, Doctor?'

She turned. There was John, looking efficient and alert in his scrubs. A tiny, aberrant part of her mind said that he also looked… No! She had work to do.

'See if you can find a kit to make a preliminary examination,' she said. 'You know, stethoscope, sphygmomanometer, thermometer and so on. Then start a set of case notes, ask Gary here what he did, what dosages he gave and if possible when he gave them.' She pointed to Peter, the man with the badly broken leg. 'And then we need a giving set for this man. He needs plasma expander and he needs it urgently. Also, can you give him oxygen?'

She knew she didn't need to specify how or what to give, she had every confidence in John.

She turned to the other man. 'Gary, when you've finished talking to John here, will you wait outside?'

'Glad to,' said Gary. He was obviously not happy in this room.

'Looks like your basic kit is here,' John said. He had been opening drawers as she spoke.

'Well, give me a stethoscope.' She felt happier when she had scribbled down a few case notes on a convenient piece of paper. No one seemed to be dying—not yet.

This was not one of those emergencies that required instant action without any regard for possible consequences. It was the last man, Perry, the one with the head injury, who seemed most in danger. She shone her torch into his eyes. He was concussed. She'd come back to him in a moment.

John had found the giving sets, had set up an IV line for Peter Nellist and was administering oxygen. Abbey came over and found a vein, started a drip at once. Peter had lost a lot of blood. He might also be bleeding directly into the tissues. He'd need a careful eye kept on him.

All three men had been half undressed, Abbey decided to fully undress them all. It was all too easy to find an injury later that had been overlooked. But after she and John had cut away the clothing that was left, they found nothing more. Good. But it had been important to look.

'Someone had a bit of a heavy hand with the painkillers,' John observed. 'These two men are well out of it.'

'True. So let's take advantage of that.'

She pinched Peter's toenail for five seconds. The nail went white—and the colour did not return for a further five seconds. Poor capillary refill. There was some kind of obstruction to the flow of blood, and if she didn't get it fixed Peter might lose his foot—or even his leg.

'We need to get this leg straightened. Do you think there might be an inflatable splint somewhere?'

'There's bound to be,' John said. 'I think broken bones might be quite common on a rig.'

He looked at a list fixed to a cupboard door, opened it. 'Yes, here we are.'

'This could hurt him,' Abbey said. 'I'm relying on him prescribing himself enough morphine to keep him under.'

John glanced at the notes he had taken from Gary. 'He prescribed enough,' he said.

The two of them carefully positioned the inflatable splint under Peter's leg. Then Abbey took hold of the foot and applied traction, carefully easing back the injured leg, reducing the fracture. She nodded to John. 'We'll hold him like this.' John adjusted the supports, inflated the splint.

'Best we can do for now,' Abbey said. How's the capillary refill?'

This time John pinched the toe. 'It's good,' he said. 'Back to normal.'

The two of them now moved over to Eric and looked at him thoughtfully. A bad pain in the arm and shoulder? She put her head round the door, saw Gary sitting outside. 'Gary, just how did Eric injure his arm?'

'He fell backwards, apparently managed to grab hold of a railing as he fell. But he couldn't hang on.'

'Thanks.' Abbey shut the door, looked at John 'Dislocated shoulder?'

John nodded. 'Sounds like it. I've put one back before, you need strength.'

Ideally they should have an X-ray but the longer they left a dislocation untreated, the harder it would be to deal with.

Abbey ran her fingers over the arm and shoulder of the now half-conscious Eric. No break that she could feel. She nodded at John. 'Dislocation. Let's go for it.'

'Does he need more painkillers?'

'I don't want to give him too much. With any luck he should be dosed up enough. Have you done this before?'

'Quite a few times.'

'Then you do it. You're stronger than me.'

They sat Eric upright. Abbey held him from behind and John extended the damaged arm. There was a moment as John felt around the injured joint. He could easily feel the displaced ball of the humerus. Then he pulled.

Eric gave a yell. 'That hurt!' he said.

'It would have hurt a lot more if we hadn't fixed it,' John told him with a cheerful smile. 'Now I'll get an ice pack to reduce the swelling and then you can try to get some sleep.'

So far so good. She had two cases she was reasonably happy about. They were relatively pain-free and their conditions wouldn't get worse. Eric might need some physio, and Peter would definitely need surgery, but for the moment both could wait.

It struck her that she was working well with John. They were a team. If she needed an instrument, all she had to do was stretch out her hand—and there it was. As if he could read her thoughts.

Could he read all her thoughts—not just the medical ones? She thought that perhaps he could. So what was he going to do about them?

She was a doctor! No time for this kind of brooding now!

Now it was time to look at Perry—and knew that this

case was probably beyond her. Carefully, she lifted the dressing on his head, felt his skull under the injury. Very little doubt. She could feel the movement of bone fragments. Perry had a depressed fracture of the skull, was almost certainly bleeding intracranially 'I'm going to need expert help on this,' she muttered to John. 'This is beyond my skill.'

'Get Gary to patch you through to a neurosurgeon,' John suggested. 'They can afford to get a surgeon on the line in minutes. The surgeon can talk you through your diagnosis, and what treatment is best.'

She looked at him in amazement. Why hadn't she thought of that? She must be getting tired. 'Good idea.' She went outside to speak to the nervous Gary, told him what she wanted.

Gary was obviously pleased to be of help. 'I think I can get hold of a surgeon quickly,' he said. 'We have an arrangement with a hospital and...' He smiled. 'We can do better than set up a radio link,' he said. 'We've got all sorts of electronic experts here. We can arrange a television camera so the surgeon can see what you see and talk to you at the same time.'

Abbey looked at him in disbelief. 'You can arrange that?'

'Within minutes,' said Gary.

In fact, it all took half an hour. And then she was standing in the smallest operating theatre she had ever seen. It was as sterile as it could be. She was gowned, gloved and masked, so was John. So, for that matter, was

Leonard, the electronics expert, who sat behind his television camera and didn't look at all happy. They needed Leonard because the surgeon had said that he needed a movable camera—one that could be brought in close to focus on details or move back for a broader view.

John had given Leonard a pill. 'This will stop you feeling sick,' he said. 'But if you do feel sick, tell us.'

'Yes,' said Leonard.

The neurosurgeon was a Mr Connelly. His voice boomed out from a box on the wall. They had all been introduced. 'I need to know whom I'm directing,' Mr Connelly had said.

Mr Connelly had taken charge. He thought that Perry needed an operation at once. 'From your observations and my experience I would say that if he doesn't have an operation to relieve the pressure on the brain, he will almost certainly die. Abbey, you will have to perform it. I will direct you.'

'I've never done anything like this before!' Abbey had shouted.

'Now's the time to learn,' Mr Connelly said. 'John, you're happy administering the anaesthetic?'

'I'm happy.'

'I've suggested a very light dose, there shouldn't be any problems. Abbey, you have all your instruments to hand? Leonard, show them to me.'

Obediently Leonard moved the camera so Mr Connelly could see the neat row of instruments, laid out ready.

'Let's begin.'

John had already shaved Perry's head. Abbey took up a scalpel. 'The first cut is always the hardest,' Mr Connolly said. 'So make it fast.'

Abbey had watched this operation when she'd been training. In a small way she had assisted. But that had been in a large theatre, with X-rays on the wall, a CT scan to refer to, a surgeon, a second surgeon, a scrub nurse, an anaesthetist.

'First we bare the scalp,' Mr Connnolly said. 'Then we start drilling. We saw off a flap of scalp, we release the pressure and we cauterise when necessary. Then we reverse the process.'

'A piece of cake,' said Abbey.

There were times when she nearly despaired, but Mr Connolly was a surprisingly good teacher. His instructions were exact and clear. If she made a mistake, he patiently showed her how to put it right.

'Put your scalpel down,' he said. 'Stand upright. Stretch your hands over your head, lean backwards. Take a deep breath. You're crouching over your patient. Keep a bit of distance.'

And then there had been John. He had muttered words of encouragement. He was masked—they were both masked—but she could tell from his eyes that he was smiling at her.

And then, in time, it was done. The finals obs were taken.

'You've done an excellent job, Abbey,' Mr Connolly said. 'I must confess, I wasn't too sure you could do it.

But we had to try. And you did do it. It's been good working with you, we must do this again some time.'

'No we mustn't,' Abbey said. 'If there is another time, I want you leaning over my shoulder in person.'

'You did well, you've got the touch. If you ever feel like a career in surgery, come and see me. Good morning, all.' And the connection was cut.

'He said good morning,' Abbey said vaguely to John.

'It's half past one. You've worked a long day, Abbey.'

She had never felt more tired. She stood, turned to leave the little room. She said, 'That's what doctors do. But now we can all have a bit of a rest. There must be a bunk for us somewhere, I'll go and ask Gary. But we'll need to keep up obs on Harry and Perry here. You do the first couple of hours and then I'll—'

Finally fatigue caught up with her. She tripped, fell, had only the strength to put out one feeble arm to steady herself. Her head smashed against the steel bulkhead and she was instantly unconscious.

She was still exhausted but now her head hurt as well. And someone was messing with her eyelids. She opened them, stared vaguely at John. He was leaning over her, looking anxious. There was a small torch in his hand. 'What are you doing?'

'I'm checking to see if you're concussed. I don't think you are.' His voice was hoarse. 'Abbey, you terrified me when you fell. I could hear…' Then he stopped and she knew he was trying to reassure her, to act like a medical professional. 'You're going to have a headache and there'll be swelling. But I don't think it's too serious. How do you feel?'

Abbey wanted to sleep. It was hard just trying to work out what he meant, what she had to reply. She wanted to sleep. And her head hurt. Oh, and there was another pain. She'd almost forgotten it. 'My arm,' she said.

She felt take her arm, run fingers up and down it. It made the pain come on more strongly. 'That hurts,' she said. 'Where am I?'

'Your arm hurts because I think you've fractured it. Quite badly. And you're lying in one of the bunks here. Now I've got four patients.'

'I'm not a patient. I'm the doctor.'

He put an arm behind her, eased her forward. 'Drink this,' he said.

She did, and he gently let her down again. 'Painkiller and sleeping mixture,' he explained. 'Now you can sleep.'

No, she couldn't. She had patients to deal with… Her eyelids closed again.

Something rather nice was happening to her. Whatever it was, she was enjoying it. She wasn't quite sure what it was but, yes, it was rather nice. What was it? She was only half-awake but she knew what it was. She was being stroked. Someone was stroking her hair and then letting his fingers trail down her face, caressing her cheeks, teasing the corners of her mouth. Yes, it was rather nice. Who?

Then she came fully awake and the world was a harder place. Her head hurt and her arm hurt and she had three injured men to look after. She opened her eyes and there was John.

'What time is it?'

'Half past seven in the morning,' he told her. 'And after yesterday's storm, it's going to be a fine day.'

Half past seven? What had happened to the night? 'What about my patients?'

'All doing well. They won't be your patients much longer. The weather's better and there's a helicopter on the way, bringing a doctor and a nurse. They're going to take you all back to hospital in Aberdeen.'

'I'm not going to Aberdeen!'

'I'm afraid you are. First, I want to make sure that your head is OK. Second, I've strapped up that arm of yours as best I can, but I'm pretty sure that it's a compound fracture. You're going to need to see an orthopaedic surgeon. Probably the same one as Peter Nellist.'

She looked round the tiny ward, saw the other three bunks. One man was sitting up—Eric, the man who had dislocated his shoulder. 'Hi, Doc,' he called. 'Next time you're ashore I'll buy you a drink.'

'With this head I don't think that I ever want to drink again.'

She looked back at John, saw the fatigue in his eyes. 'Are you coming ashore, too?'

He shook his head. 'The *Hilda Esme* is coming to pick me up as the sea is a lot calmer today. We'll be diving later.'

'What happened after I hit my head?'

He shrugged. 'I coped. I've done two-hourly obs,

they're all filled in on the forms. No problem. I slept in this chair. I was worried about you, Abbey.'

'Just a bruised head and a broken arm,' she said. 'I'll survive. But I'm sorry you're not coming ashore with me.'

She knew she was not making sense. Thoughts were buzzing round her head. She was worried about her patients, although she knew there was now no need. She was worried about John, he ought to be coming with her. But why? She was worried about her arm, she needed that for work. And what about her job on the *Hilda Esme*?

Something of her panic must have shown on her face. John leaned over, smoothed the hair from her face. 'Don't worry,' he said, 'there's nothing more to worry about. In fact—hear that?'

She could hear a distant noise that was getting louder. 'Helicopter,' John said. 'It'll take you back to the mainland.'

'But, John, I…' She felt that there was something of great importance she had to tell him, but she didn't know what it was so she closed her eyes. It was easier that way.

The noise of the helicopter got louder, and then diminished. She was vaguely aware of John going to the door of the sick bay, and then there were other people in there with him.

'I'm a doctor, not a patient,' she said when someone began to take her pulse.

'At the moment you're both,' a kindly voice said. 'I'm Dr Masters and this is Nurse Tanner, and we're going to take you to Aberdeen. Now, if I can just have a quick squint at that head of yours…'

She found it surprisingly easy to be a patient. All you had to do was lie there, not worry and let someone else do all the work. She half heard a whispered conversation between John and Dr Masters and knew it was about her. She didn't care. She'd be taken care of.

It was a bit different when she had to be moved. She was carefully lifted from her bunk onto a stretcher, wheeled down a corridor, through a lot of doors and into a large lift. Then out into the open air—and it smelt so good.

She had one last glimpse of the oil rig's towers soaring above her and then she was neatly inserted into the body of the helicopter. Nurse Tanner carefully strapped her in and then went to fetch the other patients.

Nothing for Abbey to do. She might as well go to sleep.

The short helicopter journey could have been a bit of an adventure, but she slept through most of it. She was shaken awake for a moment when the noise became nearly intolerable and they lurched into the air. But then she slept again. Only when she was unloaded in the hospital grounds did she fully wake up.

'I feel that they're still my patients,' she said to Dr Masters. 'I know they're out of my hands, but how are they doing?'

'Two of them very well,' he replied. 'The man with the depressed skull fracture—he's seriously but not dangerously ill. But for you he would be dead.'

'Right,' said Abbey.

John stood on the pad, watched the helicopter's juddering rise, saw it half circle the rig and then set off for shore. He felt that its departure symbolised the end of something for him. He felt tired and desolate.

For a moment he relieved the horror of the moment when Abbey had slipped. He had known just how tired she had been the night before. She'd had a long day before they'd got wet through in the cage, being hoisted up onto the rig. While she had been operating on Perry she had managed to run on adrenaline. He had seen it happen before. People could summon up unexpected reserves of strength when the situation demanded it, but afterwards there was the inevitable payback.

Abbey had paid back. Once again in his mind he saw her slip, saw the feeble attempt to save herself, heard the sickening crunch as her head hit the metal bulkhead. He remembered his horror as she'd lain on the floor. He had thought she was dead.

He had wanted to tell her something of this, of how he had felt. But somehow, when they had a few minutes together and she was awake again…the words just had not come.

And now she had gone. He had a dull suspicion that she had gone out of his life for ever.

CHAPTER NINE

'It's just a fractured humerus! A broken arm!' Abbey looked at the orthopaedic consultant in horror. 'When I worked in A and E we used to turn those round in an afternoon. Get them in a cast, give them painkillers and send them home. I don't need an operation!'

The consultant waved the X-rays at her. 'You didn't turn compound fractures like this round in an afternoon. I want you in Theatre this afternoon, and it's going to be quite a long stretch as the arm needs to be pinned. Afterwards…well, a stay of a few days before you're discharged. And then you take things easy. No way do you go back on a ship.'

'But I'm the ship's doctor.'

'What kind of a doctor will you be with one arm?'

It was a powerful argument. 'I'll do whatever you say,' she said.

'Right. Start by signing this consent form.'

Abbey sighed and signed.

She'd never stayed in a hospital for long. Not as a patient, that was. It was odd, seeing things from a different point of view. Little things became important—like the daily visit by the consultant or the arrival of her morning cup of tea. And the consultant had been quite stern about one thing. 'Remember, you are a patient now, not a doctor. If you see something you think needs putting right, tell a nurse. Don't try and diagnose the people who come in here. And I'll give you a word of warning—don't tell any of the other patients that you are a doctor. If you do, you'll spend hours listening to complaints about which you can do nothing.'

'I'll remember that,' she said.

On the second day of her stay she phoned her brother in Florida. First of all he said he would fly over to see her. When she persuaded him that it wasn't necessary, he made her promise to come over to visit and recuperate as soon as she was able. She did promise and she intended to go. It was something to look forward to.

On evening of the third day she had a visitor— Captain Caleb Farrow. He brought two bunches of flowers, one from the salvage firm and one from the divers and crew. 'We're coping but we're missing you,' he said. 'The ship isn't the same without you on board.'

'I'm missing both the crew and being on board,' she told him. 'But I'd better tell you now. I can't see myself being able to work for another three or four weeks. And by that time the job will be over.'

He nodded. 'It will. And I gathered that you wouldn't be able to return, so that makes this bit of my job easier. I have to tell you that the company has decided to lay you off at once. You will, of course, be paid your full salary for the contract. There will be a handsome bonus—apart from anything else, the company billed the people who run the oil rig. You'll get a letter telling you all this, and also asking if you'll be available for work in the future.'

Abbey was silent. She had always known this was a temporary job—but now it was ending she felt very sad. 'So I'll never board the *Hilda Esme* again?' she asked.

'If you ever find yourself near her, you know I'll always be pleased to see you,' he said gruffly. 'I remember you jumping into that cage at the side of the rig. Took a lot of guts to do that.'

'Just my job,' she said. 'It's been good working with you, Captain.'

When he had gone she felt lonely, something she hadn't felt for some time now. And the thought that had been evading her—or she had been evading—came to haunt her. What about John?

He hadn't come to visit her—he could just have managed it in an evening. He hadn't written to her, even sent her a message. It was as if everything that had been between them was now to be forgotten.

She remembered their last few desperate hours together when they had jumped into icy seas to board the oil rig, treated two men and performed an operation on a third that had saved his life.

At the time she hadn't thought about it but now she recollected that they had made a good team. John knew what she was thinking, could anticipate her actions.

And she knew that, whatever she did, John would be there to support her.

For those few hours they hadn't thought about each other, they had just been together. Then she remembered how, in the morning, she had regained consciousness, feeling the touch of his fingers on her face. She thought there had been love in that touch.

So now she could admit it to herself. She loved John. She had told him once that she nearly loved him but had stopped short at that. That was exactly how she had felt then. But now things were different. She knew that she loved him and she doubted if she would ever again find another man like him.

A pity he didn't—or couldn't, or wouldn't—love her. So what should she do?

Perhaps he had no real feelings for her. But she doubted that. There was something between them that both recognised. Finding out about Mick had almost torn them apart. Perhaps it was a measure of their regard for each other that they could both put it behind them. And she felt that although they had kept their distance for a time, they had drawn closer again.

One thing she knew. She had gone as far as she dared, as far as was proper, in showing her own feelings. Now it was up to him. 'Tell me you love me,' she muttered to herself.

The next morning she phoned the McElvey Centre. The manager was pleased to hear from her, anxious to do whatever he could to help her. Yes, he could get one of the female members of staff to go into Abbey's room and pack all her belongings. Yes, he could load them into her car and arrange for someone to drive it to the hospital. And he hoped that Abbey would visit them again some time.

'I've been really happy with you,' Abbey assured him.

The car arrived the next day. She could walk around the grounds now so she took what she wanted out of the car and arranged for it to be garaged until she needed it. Then she settled to wait.

Three days until she was discharged from the hospital. John would know at once that her car and belongings had been taken to her, gossip would see to that. From the captain he would learn that she would be in hospital until the end of a week. So it was up to him. He could visit her, he could write to her, he could phone her.

She waited, hopefully at first and then with increasing despondency. John didn't get in touch. The last afternoon she sat in the hospital garden with her mobile phone, making enquiries and arrangements. And at the end of the afternoon the next step in her life was ready.

She would book into a hotel for a couple of days. When she left they would garage her car for as long as she liked and store her surplus baggage. She would go to Florida to stay with her brother and his family— all she needed was a light case. She would fly from Aberdeen down to Glasgow and then cross the Atlantic from there. When she came back to Aberdeen—when she could drive again—the *Hilda Esme* would be long gone. As would all those who sailed in her.

The consultant signed her out of hospital, but cautioned her against trying anything too strenuous. He told her that Perry, the man she had operated on, was making a full recovery, thanks to her. Abbey took a solitary taxi ride to the hotel.

She was making herself look forward, and had told herself that she would start a new life. Her first attempt at a new life had been a bit of a disaster, but she had learned.

Next morning she reminded herself that she had decided to be the master—or mistress—of her own fortune. She would do what she liked, not what chance— or good sense—forced on her. She would go back to Dunlort for one last visit.

A taxi took her there and she asked the driver to stop on the hill looking down on the little seaport. She got out to look, and frowned. The *Hilda Esme* was in harbour. So was the great barge that had carried the rescued drums of fuel to the quayside. Evidently the divers' job was done and all the drums had been recovered. Abbey pursed her lips. She didn't want to meet any of her old friends. Not really.

She asked the driver to set her down near the town centre, told him that she would phone his firm if and when she needed a lift back. Then she decided not to go down to the harbour. She would walk to where she had spent so many peaceful hours—and so many earth-shaking ones, too. She walked along the clifftop path to her eyrie.

It was pleasant to sit there. There was the castle she had wondered about so often. In the other direction there was the harbour, but she could see the *Hilda Esme*.

She sat there, feeling melancholy. So many of the great memories of her life had occurred here—even though she had been here so seldom. She wondered where she would be in a year's time, where her life would lead her. Would she meet another John? She doubted it.

Then there was the rustle of bushes, the sound of feet sliding down over the stones. And someone walked into her eyrie. 'Hello, Abbey,' John said.

He looked both the same and different. There were still the darkest blue eyes she had ever seen, the unruly hair, the obvious but understated muscles. The same casual clothes—white chinos and blue polo shirt. But something had changed about his face. It looked thinner and there was a more wary look to his eyes, as if he had just discovered some sad truth.

'What are you doing here, John?'

He shrugged. 'You were seen in town. You know what gossip is like around here, I was told practically at once. And I knew you'd come here. You don't…mind me coming?'

'Not at all,' she said politely. 'Why don't you sit down?' She moved along the stone slab to make room for him.

He sat. 'How's the arm? I see you still have to wear a sling.'

'My arm is fine. It was a nasty break, but it'll mend. Are you OK?'

I'm fine,' he said doubtfully, 'I'm just fine.' He seemed uneasy. 'What are your plans for the future?'

'I'm going to Florida to stay with my family. After that…who knows? I have things to sort out in London and then I thought I might apply for a job here.'

'Here?'

'In Scotland.'

What is wrong with us? a voice inside her screamed. *We both feel the same thing, and yet here we are making bland and boring conversation like a couple of casual acquaintances. We were lovers! We risked our lives together!*

But all she could say was, 'Where are you thinking of working?

'I've been offered jobs in Australia and the Gulf. Both sound good. And I've even been offered a place here in Scotland. The money isn't that good but the job is permanent.'

Conversation seemed to die out. He looked at her with such obvious yearning that she knew exactly what he was feeling. But how to get him to say anything?

She looked down, then stooped and eased back the cuff of his trousers. Just touching him gave her a thrill, and some confidence. She looked at the little M dot tattoo on his ankle.

'Mick was so impressed that you had finished that race,' she said. 'I think I will be. Tell me about it.'

He looked at her, frowning. 'Why do you want to know?'

'I'm just curious. Tell me about the race and I'll know a bit more about you.'

He didn't ask her why she should want to know more

about him. He gazed out to sea and said, 'I'll tell you if you want. I think it's the hardest race in the world. And it took more out of me than I thought I had.'

She found it interesting to watch him as he told the story. He seemed to be going back, reliving the experience. And she felt the passion he had felt.

'It takes place in a place called Kona, in Hawaii. Two thousand people take part, but not all of them finish. You start with a two-and-a-half-mile swim. It's important to get off to a good start. Then there's a one-hundred-and-twelve-mile bike ride. And when you've finished that, the normal twenty-six and a bit miles marathon.'

Abbey winced. She had once been a race doctor for a marathon, knew what it could do to a man. But a swim and a bike ride as well!

'It's even worse than it sounds,' he went on. 'For a start, Hawaii is very humid. You sweat and drink, sweat and drink. Then there's the temperature—around ninety degrees. It's all lava fields there, the heat is reflected off the rock and beats on you. And for the bike ride, you pedal out to a point and then come back. Usually there's a wind against you, going out. And often it changes, so that it's also against you coming back.'

'How long did it take you?'

'Thirteen hours, twenty-seven minutes and forty-eight seconds. I mention the seconds because they hurt, too.'

'All you've told me is what you did,' she said. 'Now tell me what you felt.'

'What I felt?'

'Any long race is won by a combination of physical

and mental—or spiritual—strength. I heard that in a lecture given by an Olympic marathon runner. So tell me what you felt.'

'I don't like talking about my feelings!'

'I know,' she said, and waited. Her heart was pounding, but she managed to look calm.

Eventually he started, speaking slowly, as if reliving the experience. 'I was well trained,' he said. 'I'd trained for two years, a minimum of seventeen hours a week training. So when I started things were easy, I enjoyed myself. That feeling goes on until you're about halfway through the course. Then you realise that you've got to do again what you've just finished. And it hurts. After that things get worse. And you're right—it's not physical, it's mental. You're not really out of breath, your legs will carry on. But everything seemed desolate, pointless. And you don't know why you're doing it. Towards the end of the race you're in hell, your body is seizing up and your brain seems to be shutting down, too. Nothing matters.'

He was silent for a moment then he added, 'But you don't stop.'

'And it was the hardest thing you'd ever done?'

'It was more than that. It was the hardest thing I could ever imagine doing.'

'Right,' Abbey said. 'John, if you can put your body and brain through torture like that, why do you find it so hard to tell me what you feel about me?'

'What?'

'You know what I'm talking about!' She turned to

him, grabbed one of his arms and shook him. 'You knew I'd be here. Why did you come, too? And don't give me some old rubbish about saying goodbye to a shipmate because that just won't do. And why didn't you come to see me in hospital?'

'I thought…I thought you wouldn't want to see me.'

'That's a lie and you know it! I was desperate to see you. I kept remembering when I woke up on the oil rig and you were stroking my face. I wanted you there at the hospital and you didn't come to see me.'

She was angry now. And when she saw the concern on his face she grew angrier still. 'I didn't think there was anything left to sort out between us, but apparently there is. So we'll do it now. One. There was a possibility that I caused Mick's death by writing a letter. I'm over that, it's not a problem for me. Is it for you?'

'Well, no…but I—'

'No buts. Two, you know you're not responsible for Mick's death and it's foolish to think you were. Right?'

'Well, yes, I suppose—'

'Three. Mick is dead. His widow and his friends can carry on with their own lives.'

'Yes,' he said. 'Abbey, I'm over all that and I—'

'Four. You say you're a loner. Perhaps you are. But there is an alternative, and you can choose it if you want.'

She stood. 'I'm going now. Once I'm on the cliff path, I'll be out of your life for ever, we'll never meet again. If there's anything you want to say to me to stop me, now's your last chance.'

She was starting the climb up the cliff face before he

spoke. Her heart was hammering. She had risked everything on one throw of the dice—and it looked as if she
had lost.

'Abbey, please, don't go.'

She stopped, but didn't turn. 'Why not?'

'Because…' There was a pause that could have been
measured in seconds or in years. 'Because,' he said, 'I
love you.'

Now she turned, walked the few paces back to where
he was standing. 'That wasn't hard, was it?' she said.
'But you must practise, say it to me every day. And I
love you, John Cameron, I'll tell you every day.'

Only then did he kiss her. And after a minute or two
she said, 'Tell me again.'

'I love you, Abbey Fraser.'

'Good. Now, it's hard getting undressed with your
arm in a sling. Could you undo my dress?'

They lay there, warmed by the sun. He had his arm
round her, she was snuggled into his shoulder. 'If you
want to wander, then I'll wander with you,' she said.
'We can go anywhere in the world.'

'I've seen the world. How about wandering as far as
Scotland? I've been offered a job in a diving school.'

'Sounds good to me. Do you think they'll need a doctor nearby?'

'It's possible,' he said. 'Now I think everything's
possible.'

MILLS & BOON®   0206/03b

Live the emotion

_Medical
romance™

THE SURGEON'S PREGNANCY SURPRISE
by *Laura MacDonald*

At a friend's wedding, Chrissie Paige falls for the best man – fellow surgeon Sean O'Reagan. After one passionate weekend together they go their separate ways. Chrissie can't stop thinking about him. Then she finds that not only is Sean her new boss, but she's pregnant with his child!

A FRENCH DOCTOR AT ABBEYFIELDS
by *Abigail Gordon*

When Dr Giselle Howard arrives at Abbeyfields she has no intention of leaving her Parisian lifestyle behind. But the welcome she gets from the villagers, not to mention the affection she has for local GP Marc Bannerman and his two young children, creates a bond she can't ignore…

Abigail Gordon charms us with her enchanting depiction of the warmth and community of English village life

IN HIS LOVING CARE by *Jennifer Taylor*

Lewis Cole's life has changed in an instant – he has a daughter! No longer single city surgeon, he's single father and country GP. He's determined to give little Kristy all the love she needs, but there's also room in his heart for beautiful Dr Helen Daniels. Helen, however, needs more – a child of her own…

Bachelor Dads – Single Doctor… Single Father!

On sale 3rd March 2006

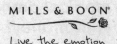

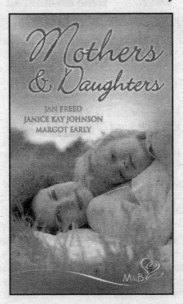

FREE

4 BOOKS AND A SURPRISE GIFT!

We would like to take this opportunity to thank you for reading this Mills & Boon® book by offering you the chance to take FOUR more specially selected titles from the Medical Romance™ series absolutely FREE! We're also making this offer to introduce you to the benefits of the Reader Service™—

- ★ **FREE home delivery**
- ★ **FREE gifts and competitions**
- ★ **FREE monthly Newsletter**
- ★ **Books available before they're in the shops**
- ★ **Exclusive Reader Service offers**

Accepting these FREE books and gift places you under no obligation to buy; you may cancel at any time, even after receiving your free shipment. Simply complete your details below and return the entire page to the address below. You don't even need a stamp!

YES! Please send me 4 free Medical Romance books and a surprise gift. I understand that unless you hear from me, I will receive 6 superb new titles every month for just £2.75 each, postage and packing free. I am under no obligation to purchase any books and may cancel my subscription at any time. The free books and gift will be mine to keep in any case.

M6ZEE

Ms/Mrs/Miss/Mr..Initials ....
BLOCK CAPITALS PLEASE

Surname ....

Address ....

....

....Postcode ....

Send this whole page to:
The Reader Service, FREEPOST CN81, Croydon, CR9 3WZ